SICK BOY

By Sean Waller

First published by Dog Ear Publishing
4010 W. 86th Street, Ste H
Indianapolis, IN 46268
www.dogearpublishing.net

dog ear
PUBLISHING

ISBN: 978-145750-148-7

This book is printed on acid-free paper.

Printed in the United States of America

1983, B.C. (Before Cancer)

Wednesday, September 28, 1983

"Oh, God, Mikey, don't do it." That's what I said to myself as I watched Mike finish constructing his signature paper airplane and begin to line up the flight path toward our science teacher, Mr. Rudolph. To be honest, though, I wanted Mike to throw it. I wanted to see the class's reaction, and I wanted to see if Mr. Rudolph, a rumored alcoholic who was barely "there" even when he was there, would even *have* a reaction.

As Mike pulled his arm back to throw, I cringed. If his accuracy with the paper airplane was half as good as it was with a football, there was no way he was missing Rudolph. I've seen Mike throw a football before. I've been on the receiving end of hundreds of his perfect spirals. He's good, real good. Dan Marino good. Next year, when we get to high school, he'll probably skip the freshman and JV teams and go right to varsity—if, and it's a *big* if, he can keep out of trouble.

Mike actually stood up to get the perfect flight pattern. For dramatic effect, he raised his finger, checking the wind. Then, a gentle release. As Mr. Rudolph, glasses hanging on his allegedly alcohol-enriched red nose, continued obliviously reading aloud from the text, the entire class watched with anticipation. It was like watching a slow-mo version of a 50-yard touchdown pass. In my head, I could hear the NFL Films music playing as the plane headed west over the heads of students, took a right turn, and then headed due north toward its intended target. On its final approach, the plane soared over the seed projects, most of which were barely finished yet received an A anyway—Rudolph the Red-Nosed Teacher never spent time actually grading the projects.

Inexplicably, the plane rose over Rudolph's head and made a U-turn. As it was about to hit Rudolph in the back of the neck, I covered my eyes and peeked out through a narrow slit in my fingers.

Direct hit! The nose of the plane hit Rudolph square in the back of the neck.

I waited for the eruption of hoots and hollers from the class. Instead, I saw Mr. Rudolph swat the plane away as if it were a fly. Other than swatting, he didn't even move. He just continued reading from the text. Rudolph's non-reaction elicited only a few giggles from the class. That was it. Very disappointing. The class fell back into what it usually did while Rudolph read from the text. Andy Sacks and Melissa LaCosta went back to groping each other in the back of the room. To be honest, I was surprised they'd even stopped to watch the plane ride. Vinny Zamon and Lenny Corsentino picked up where they had left off, shooting spitballs. They've actually gotten pretty good and have almost completed a spitball happy face on the window. Althea Thompson, Dara Bromm, and Dina Kaplan continued their MASH game, trying to predict who they will marry, what cars they'll have, what kind of houses they will live in, how many kids they'll have, and what careers they will have. I wondered for a brief second if I was on any of their lists, especially because Althea and I were a couple back in 5th grade—not that that meant anything in 5th grade, but still.

I looked across the room at Mike, who was sitting back with his hands behind his head and his feet up on the desk, a triumphant smile on his face. He winked at me.

"Well done, my man," I mouthed to him. I'm a people watcher by nature. I love to sit back and observe the action. I've been to the airport a few times, and although my parents complain when our flight is delayed a few hours, I love it. I could sit around and watch people for hours. I like to watch reunions coming out of the gate. I like to make mental lists of the people I'll save in the event of a crash.

With the paper-plane incident over and the boredom of 8th grade science setting in again, I leaned my head into my left hand, which was supported by my elbow, and all the noise became muted.

That's odd, I thought. I lifted my head. Back to full volume. I put my head back down. Muted. After a few more repeats, I switched hands, this time covering my right ear. No muted noise. Back to covering my left ear. Muted. I could barely hear out of my right ear.

"What the heck?" I said aloud.

After class, I met up with Mike at our adjoining lockers. He still had a huge I'm-so-proud-of-myself grin.

"Dude, I can't decide if you're a genius or an immature idiot," I said.

"I'm an immature genius!" he confirmed proudly.

"No, you're geniously immature."

"Whatever works, man. Did you ask Stephanie to the dance yet?"

"Didn't have to. She asked me this morning. Right before Victoria asked me."

"They both asked you?"

"Within ten minutes of each other."

"Damn, I wish I was you sometimes."

I countered, "Sometimes?" Mike gave me a playful shove into my locker and stomped away. "See ya tomorrow!" I yelled as he walked away. He didn't even look back. He just lifted his right arm and his middle finger as a response.

It's funny how *un*spectacular huge moments in your life can be. That anticlimactic paper-plane incident ended up saving my life.

I'm only 4'9" and barely 90 pounds. That's real small for an 8th grade boy. It's real small for an 8th grade *girl*! All the boys and most of the girls tower over me. But I'm pretty gifted athletically. I'm very quick. My older brother Evan is a high school sophomore and plays varsity baseball. He told his coach that I was an awesome leadoff hitter because I walk a lot and can steal a base almost any time. And I'm a good fielding second baseman—good range to my right and can turn a double play without fear of being taken out by the runner. Evan convinced his coach to give me a fall tryout to see if I can make the freshman or JV team. The coach agreed, and the tryout was this afternoon.

I got home from the tryout around 5:30. Evan was waiting for me in the driveway.

"So, how was it?"

"My running was awesome. Fielding was real good, too. Hitting, not so good. I got a little distracted."

"Whaddya mean?"

"Stephanie came by the field to cheer me on, and I got distracted."

"You nimrod. You never let a girl distract you during a game or practice. After the game, now, that's a whole different ballgame." Evan smiled to himself, probably thinking of some "distractions" he had. He hooks up a lot! We're a good-looking family. Even my younger brother Jeremy, who's in 4th grade, has his little "girlfriends."

"So who you taking to the dance?" Evan asked.

"Whaddya mean?"

"I saw Mike at the mall before. He said Stephanie and Victoria both asked you. I say take Stephanie. You could probably get further with her."

I blushed. Evan talks so freely about being with girls and stuff like that. For some reason, I don't. I think it's because I'm not only just 4'9" and barely 90 pounds but also relatively ...not developed. I haven't really started puberty yet. I HATE taking showers in the locker room. I'm probably the only one who still...ya know.... My 6th grade science teacher used the word prepubescent. I guess that's the word for me. I pray the girls don't know that.

"Haven't decided yet. But leaning toward Steph. I gotta go." I escaped inside and found my mom preparing dinner. Wanting to change the subject so I didn't have to think about the Stephanie/Victoria situation, I got my mom's attention.

"Mom, I can't hear out of my right ear."

"What are you talking about?"

"I mean, when I cover my left ear, I can't hear out of my right."

"Really?" She took the hot pot of spaghetti off the stove and drained it into the blue plastic strainer in the sink. "Jeremy has a doctor appointment on Saturday. I'll take you with me."

Looking back on that brief, meaningless conversation, I realize that that was the last time I remember my mom being so nonchalant about anything having to do with my health. It's one of my favorite Mom memories. When it came to my health, it was her last unblemished moment. It's like she was a kid who still believed in the tooth fairy.

Saturday, October 1, 1983

Sometimes, it's the most insignificant things you remember at very significant moments. At 12 years old, while in the pediatrician's waiting room, 10 minutes before the first potential sign of my trouble, I remember feeling empathy for the pale five-year-old girl with the flu cradled on her mom's lap, and thanking God I wasn't sick like that. Turns out I was sicker.

"Tim, c'mon, kid. We'll sneak you in." That was Dr. Stengel. He was probably in his mid-50s, with his gray, distinguished hair slicked back, white lab coat down to his knees and stethoscope draped around his neck. After Jeremy's checkup, Mom mentioned my ear complaint, and Dr. Stengel obliged. I sat on the table and retold my story.

"Well, let's have a look." He checked my left ear. Then my right. "Hmm." He went back to the left ear and then again to the right. "Mmm hmm." I couldn't decipher if that was good or bad. Or maybe he saw some yummy cookies in my ear. "Go wait in the lobby, Tim. I want to talk with your mom for a second."

Thinking nothing, I went back to the waiting room and sat next to Jeremy. Mom came out about five minutes later and hustled us out the door. In the car, halfway home, Mom mentioned in a very oh-by-the-way tone that Dr. Stengel wanted to send me to an ENT to get a second look.

"A second look at what? What's an ENT?"

"It's an ear, nose, and throat doctor. Dr. Stengel thinks he saw something, and, just to be safe, he wants us to see Dr. Shulman. We're going on Friday. Don't worry; it's probably nothing."

I believed her, and she sounded like she believed herself, too. But she had the same look that Bobby Santangelo had

had in 5th grade after he had proclaimed confidently to the class that Santa Claus was going to bring him a Millenium Falcon because he had been so good that year and our teacher, Mrs. McKinney, had explained to him that Santa Claus wasn't real. He had been crushed. He had tried to play it off like he had already known, but as I stared at him, I could tell by the way his eyes remained wide and his lips pursed that he had just been delivered a serious blow. An inherent innocence was gone, never to be had again. As she was telling me not to worry, Mom had that same look.

Tuesday, October 4, 1983

The ear issue fell easily out of my head as the Stephanie/Victoria issue stepped forward. I saw Victoria at her locker before school began. I walked up to her, and before I started to speak I got a whiff of her. She must have been wearing some kind of perfume. It was strawberryish. Or raspberryish. Either way, it was "berry" good, and it surprised me. I also noticed she had her hair off her face with a Smurfette clip. Normally, Victoria has a very mousy look—wearing glasses and straight brown hair that was shoulder length, with bangs almost to her eyes. This was the first time I noticed that she could be really cute. It almost made me change what I was about to tell her. Almost.

"Hey, Victoria, what's going on?"

"Oh, hey, Tim." Big smile. "What's up?"

"Nothing. Listen. About the dance…I'm going with Stephanie. I hope that's okay. I just—"

"Oh yeah, no problem." Did I see her wince slightly? God, I hope not. "Listen, I'll see you there. Save me a dance!" She touched my arm and then turned around quickly and walked away. I felt a bit of jealousy toward whoever she was going to end up going with.

About an hour later, I saw Stephanie coming out of the gym. She had straight long brown hair, down to the middle of her back, which she almost always wore in a ponytail. Today, she wore a red bandana as a headband, with the knot on top of her head. She was wearing a white Harley-Davidson T-shirt that she ripped into a tank top. It hung off her shoulder, revealing a fluorescent red strap. She wore a red and white, horizontally striped skirt and a thick black belt. Her skin was always deeply tanned. She was really cute. And I had two inches on her, which was rare for me. I went right up to her like a magnet.

"Steph, I'm in for Friday."

"Oh my gosh! That's so cool! You want to just meet me there?"

"Yeah, yeah. I'll meet you in the gym at seven-thirty. I'm looking forward to it."

"Me too, Tim. It's going to be so much fun!" She grabbed my hand and gave it a squeeze. Did she wink at me, too? I think so. Evan was right about her. I definitely made the right decision.

Friday, October 7, 1983

I kept replaying the tryout for the JV team in my head. I think I did better than I originally thought. I prepared the right way, picturing myself making all the possible plays a second baseman could make. That's how I prepare—I picture myself in my head making the plays. Even during the game, while the ball is being pitched, I picture myself diving to the left or running back into short center field to catch a popup or covering first on a weak grounder that the first baseman fielded.

More often than not, what I picture happens. I used to picture my idol, Willie Randolph, making all these plays, but something clicked in me to start to picture myself doing it. It has *so* helped my game. I recommend it.

We got to Dr. Shulman's office, and they called me right in. We sort of have a family connection with him. His son is my older cousin's best friend. To my mom, that means we're family. She is unbelievable at making completely random or trivial things seem immensely important. Last year, Mom and I had run into a kid my age and his mom at the mall. Apparently, this kid, Pete Mueller, and I had gone to nursery school together and had played together once, before he moved a few towns away, so when the two moms ran into each other, it was a crazy-awesome reunion. For them. Pete and I just awkwardly looked at each other and half-smiled while trying to avoid eye contact. It wasn't that we didn't like each other; it was just that we didn't know each other. We hadn't been on each other's radars in seven years. So then my mom turned to me and says, "Say hi to Pete! Go on, talk to him!" I just shrugged my shoulders at him. I mean, what was I going to say? It was a terribly awkward moment, and one that happens with my mom way too often.

My mom and Dr. Shulman started talking as if they were old friends even though they'd never met. I think the word is "yenta" in Hebrew or Yiddish. That's what my mom is—a yenta, or a gossip, or a "gets in everyone's business."

It took a full 10 minutes for the doctor and my mom to finish their schmoozing. Finally, Dr. Shulman pulled his wheelie stool close to me and said, "Okay, let's have a look." He looked in my ears and then my throat. I think I saw his eyes bug out for a second, and I assumed it was my breath. A few more looks, and then he called my mom into the hallway. Next thing I knew, we were scheduled for an appointment at Westchester County Hospital the next day for a biopsy. I wasn't quite sure what that meant, and I didn't ask. I really didn't think to think anything bad. I just went along with what the doctor told me. I guess I assumed it was still no big deal.

In the morning, both my mom and dad got into the car. That immediately raised my level of concern. I asked, hopefully, if we were dropping Dad off at work. He said, "Nope. I'm coming with you guys. I want to be there when you wake up."

Wake up? What the heck was he talking about? I wanted to ask but didn't. I was afraid of the answer.

The hospital didn't seem too scary. It was very white. The walls were white. The doctors' coats were white. The sheets and blankets on the beds were white. The only real colors I saw were the nurses' scrubs. The nurses wore all different colors of scrubs—light blue, maroon, pink, orange. One male nurse wore tie-dyed scrubs with jeans. I liked the whole scrubs thing. I made a mental note for a Halloween costume.

I had to put on a gown—ya know, the kind that was open in the back. I kept my underwear on. If they asked why, I was going to claim I didn't know if I was supposed to or not, but really it was because I didn't want them to see I hadn't reached puberty yet.

While I was lying in a stall on a stretcher bed, my parents told me that my Aunt Lila was in labor downstairs.

"Isn't that such a coincidence? That's so weird!" I could tell Mom was really into the cosmic connection of having a new niece or nephew at the same place where I was having a biopsy. I nodded. I was in a daze. I still didn't really know what was going on, and I still didn't really want to ask. Then I remembered that I had the dance that night.

"Mom, can I go to the dance tonight? I'm supposed to meet Stephanie there."

"I don't know, honey. If the doctor says so, then it's fine with me."

A doctor in a long white lab coat walked into my stall, followed by a pretty nurse in yellow scrubs. Do the different colors of scrubs mean anything? Is it weird that that answer seems more relevant to me than why I'm here lying on this stretcher?

The nurse took my arm and said, "This shouldn't hurt but a bit," as she put a butterfly needle in the vein of my right arm. She was right. It didn't hurt at all. She then connected the needle to a tube, which connected to a bag of water, which wasn't water. While she did this, the doctor, who I'd never seen before, told me the procedure was not a big deal, that I'd fall asleep in a few minutes and wake up with a sore throat. By 4:00, I'd be home and ready to go.

"Can I go to a school dance tonight?"

He laughed. "Probably. See how your throat is."

An orderly in blue scrubs pulled my stretcher and started to wheel me away. I looked at my parents, and they smiled and squeezed my hand. I think I heard them say, "I love you." I wanted to say it back, but I fell asleep. Out like a light.

An hour after I woke up, we were in the car on our way home. It was 3:00 P.M. The only question I could manage was "How did it go?"

"Well, ya didn't die," Dad said. He has a really warped sense of humor. I think he really enjoys having three sons. He likes being funny and gross. He doesn't give a second thought about burping real loud in a restaurant and then trying to blame one of us. I have to admit, I always find it funny, too.

"How do you feel?" Mom asked.

"Good. A little thirsty, but good."

"Good, all is good," she said aloud to herself.

Three hours later, I had showered, had gotten dressed, and was in the car. My dad drove. "Where does this girl live? Stephanie? Is that her name? You have to go to the door and escort her to the car, ya know."

"Dad, we're not picking her up. Just meeting her there."

"That's terrible. We should pick her up. Back when I went to school dances, you always picked up your date. It's classy. It's the right thing to do."

"It's not a date, Dad. We're just gonna meet there and, I don't know, I guess dance together."

"You plan on kissing her?"

"Dad! C'mon…"

"Well, do ya?"

"I don't know."

"Then it's a date, and we should have picked her up."

We pulled up to the school, and I hopped out. My dad winked at me, and I was both disgusted and kind of encouraged. I saw Victoria amidst the crowd of kids milling around the outside of the school, hanging with her girlfriends. She looked really cute! Her hair was back in a ponytail, with one long wisp of hair hanging in front of her face.

While I was debating whether or not to go over and say hi, I was practically tackled by Mike.

"*Hola, compadre!*" he said, slapping me hard on the back. "Let's go find your girl!" I followed him in, thinking it seems that everyone is more interested in what happens with me and Stephanie than I am.

We maneuvered our way in and out around the rooms—first the cafeteria, where the band was tuning up, then through a hallway and into the gym, where the 6th and

7th graders play basketball or stand around whispering to each other in small groups. The unwritten rule at the school dances is that the cafeteria is for the 8th graders to make out, hang out, and dance in, while the gym and other hallways are for the 6th and 7th graders to do their thing.

We continued to make our rounds, and I finally saw Stephanie at the open side door of the gym. She was with a group of four girls, and she looked beautiful. She also looked out of place. She looked older, like she belonged in high school. As I got closer, I saw why. Stephanie had a high side ponytail, which kept her hair out of her face, and I could see she was wearing a lot of makeup. And lipstick—a light brown, glittery lipstick. I honestly don't know if that made me more interested in her or less. The whole moment was making me feel like I was out of my league, something I wasn't used to.

"Hey, Steph."

"Hey, Timmy!" She grabbed my hand and kissed my cheek. It left a lipstick tattoo, and I was a little grossed out.

Now, let me clarify something. I've made out with girls before. Over the summer, I was at a beach party with a bunch of people I went to camp with. We had all paired up on the beach and played a kissing game. Alley-Oop, it's called. There were six boys and seven girls. Basically, we lined up like an assembly line, boys and girls facing each other. The extra girl said, "Go!" Everyone started making out with the person across from them. After about five or ten seconds, the extra girl said, "Alley-Oop!" Everyone froze mid-kiss. If anyone laughed or moved, they were out. Most people ended up laughing and the game lasted about 30 seconds at most. Then the girls rotated and we made out again with new partners. I made out with seven girls that night. This game was so much better than Spin the Bottle. Spin the Bottle was so 5th grade.

So I wasn't completely inexperienced. It's just that the camp game was more fun. Just my friends and I having a good time. No pressure. This Stephanie thing had been building up momentum, and it was becoming too pressurized. Pressure on the baseball field, I could handle. Here, I wasn't sure I liked it.

Stephanie said, "Let's go inside. It's getting chilly out here." She took my hand, and I followed her. Mike winked at me. It was pretty cool, I have to admit, walking through the crowd, holding hands with a girl and knowing that everyone who saw us knew we were going inside to make out—until I passed Victoria right in the doorway of the cafeteria. I pretended not to see her, but I know she saw me, and I swear I think I saw a slight cringe of disappointment. Not jealousy. It was as if she wasn't mad that I was with another girl. She was just disappointed it was Stephanie.

Stephanie and I made our way into the cafeteria. The band was awesome! We jumped around, singing a few AC/DC songs with them. Then Stephanie pulled me aside and whispered in my ear, "So, are we gonna kiss or what?" She was so aggressive!

"Yeah, umm...of course. Let's go...over here."

I pulled her to the back wall, where there were already about eight couples making out. When someone got to the back wall, they'd entered a new social status. I leaned against the wall, and Stephanie looked up at me, biting her lower lip. She really was gorgeous.

She took her jacket off, and I noticed she was wearing a very thick, furry, bright yellow sweater. And something about that sweater made me want to vomit. Or maybe it was something about the moment, and I was just blaming it on the sweater. Stephanie closed her eyes and tilted her head to the right. I leaned in, and we kissed. Then we opened our mouths and we made out. And mostly, it was good—real good! But then my hands started rubbing her sweater and I was mortified by the feel of it. I became very self-conscious and opened my eyes, looking around at who was watching while we kissed. I was praying Victoria wouldn't walk by while we were on the back wall. I was hoping people were watching and that I looked cool. I was trying not to skeeve about the sweater. I was trying to be a good kisser. And all this was distracting me from just closing my eyes and enjoying the moment. I couldn't seem to get past the sweater, and the lipstick, and the makeup, and finally, I stopped and led Stephanie out of the cafeteria, using food as an excuse.

By the end of the night, after three more brief make out sessions on the back wall, each one more awkward and distracting than the previous, I had had enough. I told Stephanie that Mike and I had been challenged to a basketball game in the gym by some 7th graders and we had to put them in their place. She looked at me like she couldn't believe I'd rather play basketball than make out with her. And I agree. I can't believe it either.

I made some lame excuse. She turned to walk away, and as the yellow sweater turned the corner, I felt a huge sigh of relief build in me. I went to the gym and, on my own, played some dominating basketball with a few 6th graders. This was more my element. I wasn't as ready for Stephanie as everyone, including me, had hoped I was.

Tuesday, October 11, 1983

I believe in yin and yang, opposites balancing each other out. What goes around comes around. Even-Steven. It's fate's way of not letting you get too full of yourself or too down on yourself.

My gym teacher, Mr. Villone, called me into his office at lunchtime and told me that I had two options. He had spoken with the JV coach up at the high school. I could play JV baseball in the spring. The coach had loved my tryout and thought I'd be a great leadoff hitter and second baseman. I might not play much right away, but he wanted me on the bench to experience the team and maybe get in a few games. The other option was that I could DEFINITELY be THE starting second baseman and leadoff hitter on the freshman team. Mr. Villone even told me, only half-jokingly, that the varsity coach wanted to use me as a pinch runner. Mr. Villone told me to go home, talk to my parents, and let him know by Friday.

Feeling very psyched, I leapt off the bus, bounded up my driveway, and burst through the front door with an imperious, "Hey everybody! Guess what!" Mom and Dad were sitting together in the den on the couch, knees touching, fingers intertwined, and hands on my dad's thigh. Very meek smiles tried to permeate their grave faces.

"Come sit with us a minute, Tim."

"Did Mr. Villone call you and tell you? I'm so psyched! I think I'm leaning towards JV, although I'd get more playing time and experience with the freshman team. But maybe I'd get more experience and advice from the JV guys. It's such a tough call. What do you guys think?"

My mom butted in, "Timmy, sit. We have to talk with you."

"I know. This is a really big decision."

"No, hon. We're not talking about baseball."

"Then what?"

Mom nervously continued, "Well, it's about, umm…" She bit her lip.

Dad interrupted. "You have a tumor, kid. It's a cancerous tumor. I can't make it any softer for you. Now sit down, and let's talk."

For the next 35 minutes, they told me about the call they had received from the hospital. The results of the biopsy showed that I had a malignant tumor in my upper palate, which is like the back of the roof of my mouth. The tumor was fast-growing, and I needed to start chemotherapy and radiation treatments immediately.

There were more details. I just sat quietly while my dad told me that Friday morning we were going to Sloan-Kettering Hospital in New York City. I was going to have an operation to put two tubes in me: one in my stomach and one in my chest. The stomach tube, a gastrostomy tube, would be a direct line to my stomach, and that was how I was going to have to "eat" shortly because the chemo and radiation would essentially close my mouth for about six months. The chest tube, a broviac, was where all my chemo was going to be administered so nurses wouldn't have to stick me with an IV every day.

There was even more, but it was way too much for me to comprehend. All I remember was focusing on my mom's quivering lower lip and a teardrop welling in her eye that somehow managed to stay put. How does that happen? I think the scientific word is cohesion. Or adhesion.

I wanted to ask a ton of questions: What is a broviac? What does "malignant" mean? My mouth closed for six months? What the hell is a gastrostomy? All I actually asked, though, was "Can I still play baseball?" That was what was real to me. The hospital stuff seemed foreign.

My dad took a deep breath, ignoring my question, and asked me if I had any other questions. I slowly shook my head. Dad nodded and said, "Okay, we'll leave you alone." He gave me a big hug and whispered in my ear, "It'll be alright. We'll get through this. I love you." Then he walked upstairs. Mom just stared at me and kept touching my face at different angles. Then she took my hands and kissed my forehead. She followed my dad upstairs, and I was left alone.

A moment later, Dad yelled down, "Mr. Villone called. I say play JV."

Friday, October 14, 1983

Wednesday and Thursday were a blur. My parents called Mike's parents, so Mike knew.

"How did this happen? Man, this sucks," he whined.

"Yeah, I'm still not sure what the hell is going on."

"Whatever you need, bro, I'm here. Except homework. I ain't bringing you homework. Can't contribute any negativeness. Only positivity."

"Are those even words?" We both laughed, but it wasn't as natural as it usually was. Without having to use words, we both knew that things were about to be different for a long time—like one of us had just been shipped off to military school or something.

My parents also called the school, so all my teachers knew. Thursday afternoon, I went to Mr. Villone and told him I wanted to play JV. He smiled, patted me on the shoulder, and said something like, "You got it," or "Great decision," or "Good call." Something contrite. As I left his office, I saw him drop his head onto his desk. I later heard that he had gone around telling people that I was the best natural athletic talent he had ever seen in his 22 years of coaching, and what a shame it was, and how cruel it was to waste all that talent, or something like that.

Friday morning, I woke at 5:30 A.M. Mom suggested I shower, something about it being the last shower for a few days or more. I now regret, although it's not something I could have really thought to do, not being aware of the "grand scheme of things," that I didn't look in the mirror before I got dressed or run my hand along my chest and stomach one last time. That was the last morning I would ever be the "me" I was born as. The last morning that my body was whole.

The last picture I have of me where I can see my body scarless is from four months earlier; a camp photo of me and a girl named Jill. She was wearing a Stars and Stripes bikini bathing suit. I was shirtless with a fluorescent yellow Ocean Pacific bathing suit, and our arms were around each other's waists, muscle-posing by the pool. That's now one of my favorite and saddest photos.

I pretended to sleep on the hour-and-a-half ride. I didn't want to talk. I was hoping to hear my parents talk about what was coming so I could get some information without having to ask questions. But they were almost as quiet as I was.

At 8:30 A.M. we arrived at Memorial Sloan-Kettering Memorial Hospital—at 68th Street and York Avenue. My dad dropped Mom and I off in front, then he went looking for a parking spot.

Mom and I went to the fifth floor. Pediatrics. Outside the elevator was a sign:

IN-PATIENT   →
←   OUT-PATIENT

We went to the right. An hour later, I was in a light-blue hospital gown with dark-blue silhouetted sailboats all over it. I should say all over the front, because the back was completely open. I had on matching hospital slippers and a thing on my head that the lunch ladies at school wore. I looked like a little kid in a bad Halloween costume. I was lying in a bed, an IV needle in the back of my hand attached to a saline drip.

Mom was next to me, holding my hand. Part of me didn't want her holding my hand; I already felt babyish enough with the gown. But most of me wanted her hand because I had no idea what to expect. I barely knew what the hell I was even here for, and I was really scared. Mom kept rubbing my hand like she was kneading dough. I looked at her and managed a weak smile. She looked back at me, nodding very quickly, as if trying to convince herself that all was okay.

The surgeon came in and sat down in between Mom and me. He started to explain what was about to happen. I was going to have a tube inserted directly into my chest, into a vein. The tube was about one centimeter in diameter and would hang about four inches out of my chest, with a clamp at the end of it. This is called a broviac, and it is where all my chemotherapy will be administered. This is so the nurses won't have to stick my arm often and make me look like a drug addict. I am going to have the broviac in for 15 months. *Fifteen months?!* The doctor told me he was going to also insert a feeding tube directly into my stomach. He called it a gastrostomy, and it would hang about a foot out of my stomach, with a clamp on the end.

"Why?"

"You're probably not going to be able to eat for a while, but you have to stay nourished."

"What do you mean?"

"The chemo is going to give you mouth sores. I'm going to be honest with you. They can be pretty painful, but we have stuff for that. Don't worry. But you'll probably be eating most meals through the tube."

I felt a tear slide down my cheek, and I tried to wipe it away. Mom reached up and did it for me.

"We're going to start administering the anesthetic now. Think happy thoughts."

"Wait a minute," I pleaded. "What if I don't really have a tumor? What if it's just a big mistake?" I started to get panicky.

The surgeon took a deep breath and very calmly handed me a mirror. "Open your mouth real wide, as wide as you can. See the back of your mouth? Back by your throat, can you see what looks like the rounded bottom of a ball or dome? That's the tumor. And that's just the tip of the iceberg. It's a lot larger than that. If you reach back, you can touch it. Maybe that will convince you it's real."

I saw what he was talking about. It was colorless, but the exact shape of the bottom of a ball. Trying not to gag, I reached in my mouth slowly with my index finger. Using the mirror, I guided my finger back until I touched the shape. It was soft, like the soft spot of a baby's head, but with the texture of a sponge. I immediately wanted to scrape it out but controlled the impulse.

The surgeon said, "I'm sorry, Tim. But it's real. And we're going to do everything we can to make it go away. It may not be pretty for a while, but it'll happen."

I watched as a nurse came in and switched IV bags. She turned a little wheel halfway down the tubing and smiled at me. I looked at Mom as she whispered to me, "I love you." All of a sudden, I felt really heavy, like I couldn't move. My eyelids were shutting, and I turned my head just in time to see my dad bounding into the room, giving me a thumbs-up. That's the last thing I remember.

When I woke up, I was feeling very groggy and weak. The first thing I noticed was my mom and dad sitting to my left. The second thing I noticed was the dreaded yellow rubber tube sticking out of my belly about five inches. It wasn't stuck to the skin of my belly like I had pictured. It was embedded *under* the skin, inside my actual stomach. The top was capped by a stopper similar to the nozzle you blow into on a blow-up raft and was taped to my chest. Then I noticed the much thinner white tube protruding from my chest, dangling about four inches down, taped against my body and capped off with a paper-clip/clothespin combo.

Mom stayed with me 24/7 for the next few days. Dad had to watch my brothers, and he had to go to work. Evan and Jeremy came to visit for a few hours on Saturday. Jeremy didn't quite get what was going on. He asked a lot of questions, more than I had. No matter what the answer was, and it was usually a sugar-coated answer, he'd always say, "Oh, okay," as he shrugged his shoulders in a no-big-deal way. Evan sat in a chair in the corner of the room just out of my eyesight. He was incessantly bouncing a tennis ball off the wall and catching it. He barely said a word other than "How ya feeling?" A few times, I caught him staring at me like a caged animal he'd never seen before in a zoo. Or maybe it was more like I was a Coney Island freak show. It made me feel weird, but I can't say I'd have done anything differently if the roles had been reversed.

Sunday, October 23, 1983

The doctor said we are going to start my chemo and radiation treatments on Wednesday. They wanted to wait a few days for the area around the tubes to heal. Apparently, infection, or the chance of infection, is watched very closely when you're on chemotherapy—something about white blood cells being low. My dad and brothers came by for a few hours this morning and left after lunch. Evan seemed relieved to leave, but Jeremy seemed disappointed.

About 4:00 P.M., our neighbor Ben came to visit. He and his wife are my parents' best friends. Ben showed up with a huge bag of food. He pulled out a fat chicken parmigiana sandwich for my mom. He put a large baked ziti, my favorite, in front of me. "I'm guessing you've had enough of the hospital food by now," he said. After getting the go-ahead from the nurse, I devoured the baked ziti. It was the best damn ziti I'd ever had!

Mom went for a walk outside after dinner. I think it was the first taste of fresh air she'd had since Friday morning. Ben sat next to me. He was the kind of guy who always had a story about something. He always knew someone famous, or knew someone who knew someone famous. Ben told me that a guy he worked with knew the promoter of a professional wrestling match that was taking place sometime soon in the city and that he was going to take me backstage to meet the wrestlers. That definitely perked me up! For the next hour or so, we talked about champion Bob Backlund, Jimmy "Superfly" Snuka, the Iron Sheik, and a new wrestler named Hulk Hogan who people think is going to be a champ one day.

An hour later, Mom came back, and Ben left. I remember thinking how cool it would be if Ben came through, but, at the same time, how grateful I was to just talk and laugh and not think about the days ahead.

Tuesday, October 25, 1983

Mike and Victoria came to visit. My mom left me alone with them. Mom was getting more comfortable with leaving me alone for periods of time. Mike came in and handed me a gift.

"Thanks, man. I appreciate—"

"It's from my mom. Before you get too thankful, it's probably one of her homemade scarves. Don't get too excited. She wanted to come up, but she is scared to park in the city, so she's double-parked out front."

I chuckled. "Man, it's good to see you."

Victoria walked next to the bed. "Hey, Tim, how are you doing?" I got the sense that when she asked the question, she genuinely wanted to know how I felt. I liked that. I liked that a lot. When my brother Evan asked, it seemed out of obligation. Not that Evan didn't care. I just felt he asked but didn't really want to hear the answer. Victoria wanted a real answer. I just wasn't ready to give her one yet.

"Okay, I guess. Ya know. I'm okay, I guess." She smiled and patted my hand.

Mike asked, "Can you walk?"

"Yeah, but umm…" I motioned to Victoria. "My gown is open in the back."

He laughed as Victoria smiled and blushed. I liked that a lot, too.

"Hey, you were really missed at Hope's bat mitzvah this weekend," Victoria said.

Mike jumped in. "Yeah, man. Everyone was talking about you. You should have heard what people thought. Vinny heard you were in a car accident. Melissa thought you were dead. She's so retarded. A few people heard you had meningitis, and Tara heard you moved to Canada."

"Seriously? Canada?"

"Yeah," he laughed. "I felt bad for Hope. No one even paid her hardly any attention."

"What did you tell them?"

"That we'd see you today and we'll tell them what's going on."

"So, what are you gonna tell them?"

"The truth. We saw you. You're in the hospital and you're doing okay. That is the truth, right, buddy?"

"Yeah." *For now*, I thought.

Victoria said, "Stephanie says hi. She told me privately that she wanted me to tell you that she is thinking about you."

"Oh, okay, thanks. That's nice."

"People were also asking about your bar mitzvah in December. They want to know if you're still having it," Mike said.

"I guess. Hadn't really thought about it, to tell you the truth."

"Mike, that's not important right now," scolded Victoria.

"I'm sorry! I'm just repeating what went on."

Victoria asked, "Are you coming back to school?"

"I think on Monday, but it depends on how I respond to my first treatments."

"Well, we hope you do."

"Yeah, I miss you, man." Mike slapped my leg with the back of his hand.

I told them about my tubes and how my body is still tender. But that was all I really felt like offering at the moment. About a half hour later, they left. The doctor came in at 2:30 P.M. to prep me for the beginning of the next day's chemo and the radiation treatments. At the end of his spiel, he told me to relax today and tonight, we were starting early in the morning.

This time, I was able to realize that today might be my last "well" day for a long time.

1983, A.D.   (After Diagnosis)

Monday, October 31, 1983

I was supposed to go back to school today, but I was too tired. I'll try again tomorrow. And I hope your Halloween was better than mine. Mine was all trick and no treat.

Tuesday, November 1, 1983

Here's what chemo is like. It's a concoction of five different medications which, when mixed together inside my body, are supposed to shrink the tumor. Four of these medications are injected directly through my broviac into my chest and into my bloodstream. For the most part, these are relatively harmless. They feel cold going in. One of them is fruit-punch red, and one of them has a weird smell. But they are not bad. The fifth medication is called Vincristine. I hate Vincristine. I loathe Vincristine. Vincristine is the root of all evil. It's given through an IV drip. A drop falls every three seconds, while I stare at it and give it the evil eye.

On the first day, after about four minutes of the Vincristine drip, I started to feel lightheaded and heavy. I remember thinking—in fact, I think I said this to my mom—that if this was what getting stoned or getting baked felt like, she should find me some pot! This was magical!

About three minutes later, I got real nauseous and had a terrible headache. It got to the point that I was only comfortable on my left side, curled up in the fetal position, looking at my mom and holding her hand. Then I started puking and I managed to say to Mom, "If THIS is what getting high feels like, you never have to worry about me doing drugs." Then I puked more. For three straight hours. I can only describe the massive headache and dizziness as what it might feel like after riding the Rotor carnival ride about 17 times in a row. Plus, I couldn't lift my head, so I had to side-puke—much of which came out my nose. And it was very messy. Finally, it stopped being messy when my stomach was empty. I dry-heaved for the last hour. I'm not sure which was worse.

I so quickly came to dread this medication that on Friday, day three, I began to visualize very evil things happening to the nurse who would administer the Vincristine.

"Okay, Tim, here's the IV. It's time," the nurse would say, trying to be sympathetic but knowing there was nothing she could say to make me feel good about this.

"Go away. I hate you."

"You can hate me if you want."

"I want to, and I do."

On day three, I counted 82 drops until the good feeling hit me. And for the next 61 drops, I smiled and prayed that this euphoric feeling wouldn't turn and become the terrible nausea. But right on cue, on the 62nd drop, I felt the headache coming on and the nausea right behind. The only positive spin I could put on this was that after about three and a half hours, I usually fell asleep for the rest of the day.

That's how I spent Wednesday, Thursday, and Friday of last week. Next, I have a week off from my chemo, during which I'll try to go to school, and then do chemo again for a week. Most of the time, I can do the chemo as an outpatient. I have to do chemo for 15 months.

Oh, and let's not forget radiation. On the Tuesday after Mike and Victoria left, I was taken to the radiation department on the second floor. I spent one hour getting my head and face papier-mâchéd so the doctors could create a mask of my face. That Wednesday morning, before chemotherapy, I had to lie on a table, my head secured in this mask. Somehow, I don't know how or when, I got two little blue dots tattooed on my face, one just underneath each earlobe. These are the targets for the laser that will radiate my skull. The mask is used to keep me super still so they can get the exact spot they needed. They zap me for about seven to ten seconds, and the smell it creates is nauseating. My dad said the smell was actually burning flesh, but I'm not sure I believe that. This process is painless, but it's scary. I'm all alone in a room, lying on my back, head secured so tightly that I can only look at the ceiling. The radiologists have heavy vests on them to protect them from the radiation—and they're in another room! I have to get 25 of these treatments.

Because I'm a little guy, I am used to standing up straight, head held high, when I walk. It gives me an air of confidence even when I may not feel it. Today was my first day back at school after being out for a week and having three days of chemotherapy and three radiation treatments. It's difficult to walk like that now. The area around my tubes is still a little sore. Plus, I'm not completely comfortable standing up straight. I feel like I'm going to pull the tubes right out of my body. I'm not, of course, but it's just a weird feeling. Maybe it's like when you put a Band-Aid across two fingers and, by pulling your fingers apart, you feel like you'll pull the Band-Aid off. Maybe not.

Anyway, I'm walking slightly hunched over. Walking through the halls back at school was weird. I had a lot of back slaps by friends, which I cringed at, because no one knows I have these tubes in me, and I was afraid someone would hit or touch one. At the same time, I was trying not to LOOK sick. I was trying to look strong and energetic. It was very difficult, and I was probably unsuccessful.

Lots of kids were staring at me. A few had heard I was dead and were quite shocked that I was walking the halls. I saw Stephanie from a distance down the hallway, and we locked eyes. She offered a weak smile. I did the same. She didn't make any effort to come up to me. I understood. It was awkward, uncharted territory. I'm not sure I would have reacted any differently if it had been her who was sick.

The rest of the week went okay, I guess. Mike was very good at noticing when I was tired, and he'd cover for me. If someone wanted to talk and he saw that I wasn't up for it, he'd jump in with, "No more questions, people! You want to talk? Have your people call Timmy's people. And no autographs, please!" Mike was my publicist/bodyguard, and I love him for that.

Victoria was real sweet, too. She would keep her distance in crowds, like in the cafeteria, but when she could catch me alone, she'd always ask how I was doing. And she'd always touch my arm the same way in the exact same spot. A gentle, caring, concerned touch. A good touch. And I like her for that.

Saturday, November 5, 1983

I woke up happy that it was the weekend and that I had a break from the celebrity of school. I also woke up not noticing that a clump of hair didn't come off the pillow with my head. I got up and trudged downstairs for breakfast. Mom was making French toast. With her back to me, I sat at the table and put my head down in my arms on the table. A few seconds later, I heard a gasp, followed by, "Oh gosh!" and then, oddly, stifled laughter. I looked up and saw that my mom was staring at me with a mix of horror and humor.

"What?" I asked.

"Oh, Tim," she said pitifully.

"What!"

Although still smiling, she teared up as she said, "Your hair. It's falling out."

"What are you talking about?" I asked as I raised my hands to my head. That's when I felt a lot less hair on my left side. I ran to the bathroom and looked in the mirror. My left side had a huge chunk of hair missing. I ran my fingers through my hair, and when I pulled them out, they were littered with hair, like the cut hairs after a haircut. I tried to put them back, realized that was very silly, and just stared.

"Son of a bitch," I said to myself.

My dad walked into the bathroom behind me and stared. I expected him to make some kind of joke about it. Instead, he said, "Tim, you got two choices. Pity yourself, or deal with what you have to deal with, head held high. You have to be able to look in the mirror and love who you see. You have to love how you feel about the person in the mirror. You are going to be bald, but you're still going to be you." He paused and then continued, "If you want, I'll help you shave it all off. Why put off the inevitable?"

And with that, he left. And I immediately got his message: Bad stuff is going to happen to me. I could just let it happen, or I could take charge of *how* it was going to happen. I could keep it on my terms. A minute later, I met him in the kitchen and said, "Let's do it." With tears in my eyes, but with confidence in my heart, I sat and let my dad shave my head bald. He shaved it so I had a thin Mohawk left.

He handed me the razor and said, "Okay, Mr. T, it's all yours."

It took me 10 minutes to muster up the courage, but I finally shaved off the last piece. I went to the bathroom and stared into the mirror. I looked like Casper the Friendly Ghost. My head was so pale. Evan and Jeremy walked in behind me. They both came up next to me and rubbed my head. I looked like a cancer patient. I felt like a cancer patient. I was a cancer patient. I started to cry and couldn't stop.

My parents came in, and all five of us hugged like we were huddling on the 35-yard line.

My dad finished the moment by finding a pen and writing on the top of my head one word. He wrote "Boo!"

The next day, I spent a few hours with a friend of my mom's. This woman, Jodie, owns a hair salon and she brought over a few wigs for me to try on. I tried on a few and settled for the one that I thought looked most like what my own hair had looked like. The wig looked terrible. If I look close, I can see the netting through the hair. The wig doesn't seem to fit right, and it actually makes me feel worse. But as bad as it looks, it is better than being bald. I mean, Mr. Clean looks cool bald. Kareem Abdul-Jabbar looks cool bald. But everyone I know has big hair, long hair, hair-sprayed hair. I feel the wig gives at least the illusion that I have hair.

By the way, when you lose your hair from chemo, ALL of your hair falls out—arm hair, leg hair, and eyebrows. I think that's what makes you look the sickest—having no eyebrows. It's very unnatural, and that, more than anything else, makes me feel freakish.

Mike came over that night to check out my new look. I kept the wig off at first. I was hoping for a confidence boost. Instead, I got the truth.

"Wow, man, you look really crappy." Mike didn't hold anything back. "I mean, I need to make fun of you right now. Can I?"

"I guess. If it makes you happy."

"You look like the alien from *Close Encounters of the Third Kind*. If I were a girl, I'd rather make out with Jabba the Hut. If I were E.T., I'd phone home and catch the express out of here rather than make out with you."

That one made me laugh. He winked at me and rubbed my bald head. Then he asked me, "Is cancer contagious? Like, can I catch it from you?"

"Are you serious?"

No answer. He just stared at me.

"I don't think so," I assured him.

"Well, it's okay if I do. We could be bald together. We'd be like a pair of walking bongo drums. Plus, *everyone* is talking about you at school. You've become even more popular than you were."

"Yeah, but it's probably in a freak-show way. Not in a way I want to be popular. Like if someone found out I wet my bed until I was nine, that would make me well known, but not in a good way."

"This is kind of a mix. I don't know."

I changed the subject. "Watch this." I pulled out the wig and put it on. I took a deep breath and waited to get slammed. "Give me your best shot," I said.

Mike studied it for a minute. He walked all around me, examining the wig from all angles, prodding it, smelling it. "It's not bad. It's passable to people who never met you before. It *feels* fake, but it looks okay. I'd make out with you."

"Thanks." Somehow, that actually made me feel better.

Wednesday, November 9, 1983

The doctors told me that I had to be admitted to the hospital for about 10 days. The chemo has knocked my white blood cell count real low. This means I am very susceptible to infection, and, apparently, having an infection while on chemo is not good. They also highly recommend that I not go back to school, probably for the whole year.

That sucks. I am going to miss my entire 8th grade! I am going to miss the Washington, DC, trip! It's an overnight trip, and legend has it that some *very interesting* things happened in the hotel, especially if a guy had a girlfriend. There have been stories about kids hitting "home runs" on that trip. Another legend was that two boys had snuck out at night, met Redskins quarterback Joe Theismann on the street, hung out with him at a Friendly's restaurant for a few hours, and gotten a ton of autographed memorabilia. Neither of these stories are probably true, but they make for some amazing anticipation over the trip.

I'm also going to miss the 8th grade dance. This is another rite of passage. It's like a mini-prom. It's the first real time guys get to go out somewhere with their girlfriends other than the diner or the movies. Everyone dresses up in suits and gowns. It's like a coming-of-age party where people transformed from kids to young adults.

I think the worst thing, though, is sports. I am going to fall far behind now with baseball. Assuming I can come back in 9th grade, a big assumption, there is no way I am starting JV. I may have to work super hard just to make the freshman team. And if I can't play until I'm a sophomore, forget it. Everyone else will have two years on me. I don't know if I can recover from that.

And here's the cherry on my cancer sundae: Mom and Dad decided to postpone my bar mitzvah, which was supposed to be on my birthday next month. I'm not mad at them. I'm just pissed at the whole situation.

Damn it, this really sucks! Instead of having an awesome year, I'll be in and out of the hospital, depending on my white blood cell count.

I was admitted Thursday morning, and that afternoon, after my chemo, which didn't include Vincristine, I got to explore a little.

I was attached to an IV drip of saline, which was just to keep me hydrated and nourished. The IV hung from a pole, which I had to drag around with me, so my pole and I took a walk around the inpatient pediatric floor.

As I walked around the fifth-floor inpatient ward with my hospital gown open in the back, my wig-covered bald head, and the pole that I had to drag around like it was a third leg, I saw some things that really, for the first time, made me realize the severity of cancer.

There were about 18 rooms on the floor, all of which had bald kids. With most of these kids, unless they had earrings, it was almost impossible to tell if they were boys or girls. Especially the younger kids. Some kids wore gender-identifying gowns—Strawberry Shortcake or Smurfs for girls, and sports, G.I. Joe, or Star Wars for the boys. Some wore gender-identifying bandanas. Almost all of them stared at me as I walked past their doorways. At first, I couldn't figure out why. Was it because I was the "new" kid? Could it be that even here, everyone sizes up the new kid, just like at school? Were they thinking, *Is he a threat? Is he cool?*

Then I thought maybe it was because they were trying to identify if I was a boy or a girl. Hopefully not! Although I was basically still prepubescent, I'd like to think I didn't look like I had girly features!

I figured it out when I passed a hallway bathroom and caught my reflection in the mirror. The reason they were staring was because I was wearing my wig. Although it was unintentional, I believe they thought it was my way of declaring that I was better than they were, that I not only had not accepted that I was a cancer kid but looked down on them. The only way I can describe the message I was inadvertently sending would be if you went to a Yankees–Red Sox game in Yankee Stadium and wore a Red Sox jersey—not out of pride for your team, but for the sole purpose of showing up the Yankees fans.

When I got back to my room, I took the wig off, gave it to Mom, and told her that I wouldn't need it here.

Just passing the other rooms for a few moments, I noticed some kids were amputees. Some were missing a leg or two, some an arm. I noticed about half the kids were sleeping. Mom told me later those were kids on their heavy chemo days. I heard a few kids crying and saw some watching TV; one having a tennis ball catch with his/her dad, and there was one empty room.

The hospital tries its best to make our crappy lives the least crappy as possible. Sloan-Kettering has an amazing playroom for the inpatient kids. Amazing is an understatement. It's like an amusement park without the rides. My mom and I went that afternoon, and if the playroom hadn't closed at 6:00 P.M., we'd still be there. In one corner, they have stand-up arcade video games. I mean, the real size! Pac-Man, Defender, Burger Time, Centipede, Donkey Kong, Galaga, and Tempest. And they were all free! We could play as much as we wanted!

Another section of the playroom was for little kids. They had hundreds of dolls, and Matchbox cars, board books, peg puzzles, and coloring books. In another part of the playroom were a pool table and a bumper pool table. Incidentally, I am an excellent bumper pool player. Our neighbors, the Fishers, have one in their basement. Paul Fisher is probably seven or eight years older than I am. I

think Evan looks up to Paul because Evan, being the oldest in our family, doesn't have that older brother role
model that Jeremy and I have. Evan goes over to the Fishers' sometimes to hang out with Paul. Paul introduced
Evan to some great music like Styx, Kiss, Yes, and Rush.
Sometimes I tag along, and while they peruse the albums,
I play bumper pool.

Best of all, the playroom has a teen room. The teen
room has a big TV, a computer, teen-level books, board
games, a pottery wheel, and a slew of science-y things. I
am not a science guy, but I certainly can appreciate the
coolness of it.

Mom noticed a sign in the playroom:

Bingo Night Tomorrow Night.
Prizes and Fun for Everyone!

Mom laughed and said, "It's just like your grandpa's
condo in Florida!"

"Yeah, complete with bald heads and people dying of
cancer." I felt bad when I said that, but Mom just looked
at me, smiled, and laughed. Then I laughed, too. As my
dad somehow already knew, Mom and I learned that we
have to have a sense of humor about the situation or else
we'll cry.

My doctors think it is best that I stay in the hospital
through the weekend to make sure my white blood cell
count gets higher. I'm bummed. I just want out of here.
It isn't completely miserable in the hospital. It is just
slightly miserable and very boring. Since I've been here,
I've had three more radiation treatments, almost puking
during one. That would have been bad because my head
was secured in the mask and I could have choked on my
own vomit. Also, the skin on the side of my face is starting

to get a shade darker than the rest of my face from the radiation. The radiation is forming a line down each side of my face, like the border between two countries on a map.

Mom tried to cheer me up with Bingo night.

"I'm not going." It's not that I don't want to go. I just want to be home. Mike told me that he and a bunch of the guys were getting together on Friday to go see *Return of the Jedi* for the eighth time.

Plus, I am nervous about having to talk with the other kids on the floor. I don't know why. I think it's because if I talk with them, they'll become real to me. I don't want them to be real. I don't want to get to know them. I don't want to be a part of all this. I just want to go to the movies with my boys back home. I'm not in denial. I'm just not ready to completely accept or embrace my situation.

It's like when my grandpa died three years ago. When Dad had told my brothers and me, Evan and Jeremy had got teary, but I had been okay. I'd had no reaction, just gotten up and walked away. I hadn't said one word about it. I had gone to the funeral, then hugged Dad, Mom, and Grandma and watched others cry. I had known it was real. I had known it happened. But it hadn't been real for *me*, in my world.

That was, until about four days later, when Mike had said to me, "Sorry about your grandpa."

I had replied, "Thanks. I can't believe he's dead." And a second after I'd said, "He's dead," the tears had started flowing and I had sobbed for a good 10 minutes. For me, the moment when I articulated the words "He's dead" was the moment it became real and I joined the "Grandpa's dead" world.

So for me, having to talk with the other sick kids will officially make me a member of "sick kid" world. And I don't want that membership card.

That afternoon, as Mom and I were finishing an Invisible Ink game of Fleet (she won again), we heard laughter coming from the hallway. Mom peeked her head out the door.

"Oh, you gotta see this, Timmy."

I joined her in the doorway, and we saw three bald little kids, one in a wheelchair, laughing and cackling as a fully made-up, balloon-making clown entertained them.

"Oh, that's so cute…" cooed Mom. I watched and smiled. Clowns are cool. So are little, laughing sick kids. Mom was right. It was a cute scene.

The clown bounced from room to room. Squeals of laughter emanated from each room, and I'm sure there were plenty of beaming parents grateful for some happiness in their children's lives for once.

When I saw the clown coming toward my room, I lay down on the bed, not hiding, but not welcoming. Like I said, clowns are cool. But they're cool when you are seven, not a month away from being 13. As the clown bounced into my room, he must have concluded that I wasn't in the mood. He immediately dropped the clown shtick and sat at the foot of my bed.

"I'm Jack. Jack the Clown. Let me guess. You're too old for clowns."

I nodded and shrugged my shoulders, not wanting to offend but not wanting to encourage.

"That's cool," he said. "I get it. From what I can tell, you're the oldest on the floor. 'Cept for Tess. She's 13 and two doors down from you. And between you and me…" He leaned in to me real close and winked. "She's a cutie. I'm just saying, ya know. Someone your age to talk to."

Mom chimed in, "Oh, that'd be wonderful!"

"Mom!"

"Stop being so sensitive. Thank you, Jack the Clown. You've cheered us up."

"That's my job, ma'am." He stood up and went back into clown mode. He did a little soft-shoe dance step, walked up to me, and said, "Take care, brother." He winked and left.

Mom said, "I'm going to peek into Tess's room and introduce myself to her mom or dad. Why don't you come?"

"No, thanks."

"Fine. Be stubborn. I'll be back." She rolled her eyes at me and left. I was mad at myself. *What the heck is my problem? In school, I have no problem talking to girls. I'm never the party pooper.* But here, I feel like my normal, happy-go-lucky personality is stuck in cement and I can't bust it out. I promised myself that I would make a concerted effort to not be such a blah.

Mom came back in the room and told me about Tess. "Tim, they're from Iowa. Her mom's name is Clara, and her grandmother is here, too. Tess's dad is back in Iowa with her two little brothers. Tess was sleeping, so I didn't meet her. I asked if they were going to Bingo night tonight and said that I would try to convince you to go."

"I'm in. I'll go."

Mom kissed the top of my head. "Good boy."

At 7:00 that night, I put on my sweatpants and my Don Mattingly T-shirt and headed down to the playroom for Bingo night. As I walked in, I saw a man who seemed very familiar. He welcomed me to the event, and I could almost place his voice. Then it hit me. It was Jack the Clown! But now, it was just Jack. He saw that I was about to acknowledge this, and he put a finger to his lips, shushing me.

"The little kids don't know, and let's not tell them." He gave me his signature wink, patted my back, and ushered me into the room. As I found a seat, I heard Jack say,

"Tess! So glad you could make it! I know this wasn't one of your better days."

"Tess never misses Bingo night. You know that, Jack," Clara, Tess's mom, replied. I looked back and saw Tess for the first time. She was small, like me. And despite her bald head, there was no denying she was a girl. She had beautiful, large blue eyes, and I could only imagine how much more beautiful they'd be if her eyelashes hadn't fallen out. She had on a way oversized, red Michael Jackson *Thriller* T-shirt and pink shorts. Tess looked tired but was making a grand effort to smile and be conversational. A few younger kids walked in behind her, and amidst screams of "Tess! Tess! Hey, Tess!" they hugged her and she patted their heads. She then looked up and locked eyes with me. She beelined through her mini-crowd of fans and sat down next to me.

"What? You never seen a bald chick before?" She surprised me.

I stammered, "No, I, umm, ya know, I just—"

"I'm just kidding. I'm Tess. You must be Tim."

Laughing, I answered, "I am. And you're obviously Tess, the mayor of Munchkin City."

"The little ones like me. What can I do? Nice hair, by the way."

"You like it? It seems to be the style in here." Tess smiled at me, and it was a big smile. A wide smile with impeccably white teeth and that showed a lot of confidence. Her eyes, though, beautiful as they were, looked tired.

"I'm glad you made it," I said rather lamely.

"I'm exhausted, to be honest," she answered, "but I try my best to not let the little guys see that I'm tired. They've kinda come to look up to me, and I want them to see me strong. For their sake, ya know?"

"I think so."

"I look at some of these kids, and they are so young. Like kindergarten or first grade or younger, and they barely even know what's going on. That keeps them positive. The little ones are so brave, probably 'cause they're so naïve. Bigger kids our age," she said as she looked directly at me and poked me. "Like YOU, seem depressed."

"Maybe because we have more of an awareness of what we're missing back home. We had 'normal,' and now we lost it. And that sucks."

"Yeah, it does, but ain't nothing y'all can do about it except be positive. Especially in front of the li'l ones. I've worked real hard to establish a standard of optimism for them. Don't screw that up!" She smiled, almost laughed, as she said that.

"I'll do my best, Miss Mayor." I smiled back.

"Okay, let's get this started," announced Jack Not the Clown. Over the next 45 minutes, all 11 kids, Tess and me included, won at least one Bingo game. We each got prizes like stuffed animals, books, or electronics. I got a Mattel handheld football game, and Tess won an electronic Simon.

When it was over, Jack announced, "Thank you guys for coming. We'll do it again in two weeks. Oh, and parents, these prizes were donated by," he looked down at a piece of paper and read, "Jefferson School in Westfield, New Jersey, in case you want to write a thank you." Jack winked at everyone and left. The other kids filed out behind him with their moms in tow.

"If you're up for it, I'll stop by your room tomorrow," I offered to Tess.

"You mean a date? Ha! Just kidding. Okay. See ya tomorrow."

I saw my mom and Tess's mom smiling at us. Oh, please—how embarrassing and unnecessary!

The next day after lunch, I wheeled my pole to Tess's room. She was sitting up, cross-legged on her bed, doing a crossword puzzle.

"Tess, hey, it's me."

"Really? I couldn't tell. Must be the new 'do."

"You love the hair jokes, don't you?"

"You're so sensitive! But you're a rookie, so I forgive you."

"Wanna hit the playroom?" I suggested.

"Sure."

We went to the playroom, and for about half an hour, she beat me at video games. Then, for the next half hour, I beat her at bumper pool.

"So, what are you in for?"

"What?"

"What kind of cancer do you have?" she asked again.

"I have rhabdomyosarcoma. Basically, a tumor in my sinuses. You?"

"Leukemia. I've been here for three months already. My goal is to make it back home to Iowa this summer for the Hobo Festival."

"What's that?"

"The second Saturday of August, we celebrate Hobo Day. Hundreds of hobos arrive in my town of Britt, set up a hobo jungle where they stay, entertain us townspeople with stories, and cook mulligan stew. That is veggie stew with just about anything thrown in. And there's always a campfire going."

"That's unique."

"Also, each hobo gives a speech about how they have spread the word of the hobos and how they've been good folk all year. Afterwards, a king and queen are elected based on who gets the loudest applause. It's really an awesome event. I'm sure it sounds corny to an East Coaster."

"No, it doesn't. Well, maybe a little. But August is a long way off. Of course you'll be back for it."

"Yeah, I know. But it gives me a goal to reach for."

"And you're always an inpatient?"

"Yeah. Too dangerous for me, apparently, to be out of my sterile environment."

"I actually just found out I can go home tomorrow. Might not be back on the inside for a while. It's like I got parole."

"I know. My mom was talking to your mom."

"Moms." I rolled my eyes as I said this.

"Here, come with me. You'll like this." We went to the playroom and met up with some younger kids—two boys about seven to nine years old and a little girl about six. Tess explained to me that whenever there is a new kid on the floor, the hair game is played. They had to try to guess what my hair looked like before it fell out, and I had to guess theirs. I guessed that both boys had had straight brown hair. I was wrong. One had had blonde curly hair and the other's hair had been black and straight. Then the four of them huddled together and correctly decided that I had had straight, short, brown hair. I then guessed that the little girl had had poofy red curly hair.

"Red curls! Yuck! Ew! No way! If I had red curly hair, I would shave it off anyway!" Tess and I laughed. The girl continued. "Guess again."

"Long blonde hair like the girl from *Poltergeist*," I offered.

"Yep!" she haughtily replied. She flipped her now-imaginary long blonde hair off of her face. "It was down to my butt!" She giggled as she said the word "butt," as did the two boys. Tess rolled her eyes at me.

On the walk back to our rooms, Tess and I talked, and it was easy talk. Not about being sick—just about normal stuff 13-year-olds talk about.

"In Iowa," I asked, "what sports teams do you root for?"

"I like the Chicago teams, the Bears and Cubs. But most people I know are St. Louis Cardinals fans. Maybe a few Minnesota Twins/Vikings fans. But everyone roots for the Hawkeyes. Go Hawkeyes!"

I told Tess about Mike and Victoria and how much I bet they'd like her.

"Is Victoria your girlfriend?"

"No. Why do you ask that?"

"The way you talk about her, it sounds like you really like her."

I'd had no idea. "If she was your girlfriend, she wouldn't have to worry about me. I'm just the hottie you're cheating on her with." She punched my arm, and we both laughed. Then it was her turn to start a conversation.

"Have you ever made out with a girl?"

"Um, yeah," I stammered, a bit surprised by the question. "A few."

"I haven't made out with any boys yet." She was so honest and matter-of-fact about her admission. Not embarrassed at all. It was a confident confession. I was impressed.

"I'm surprised."

"Why?"

"You're totally cool to hang out with. And you're very pretty."

"I know!" She laughed at herself, mocking her own answer. We arrived outside our rooms, and, with our moms nowhere to be seen, she leaned in and kissed me half on the cheek and half on the lips. It lasted an amazing five seconds.

Then she said, "I would have made out with you just now, but I can't afford the germs. But I'm going to tell my friends back home that we DID make out, 'cause in my mind, we did. Is that okay?"

"Yeah, Tess. Of course it is. I really like making out with you, too."

She giggled a bit nervously. "Yeah, well…you're leaving tomorrow, so…" She leaned in and gave me a hug. I hugged her back, and although I think I caught my mom looking at us, I didn't care.

We broke our hug, and Tess said, "I hope I never see you again."

"Why would you say that?"

"'Cause that would mean you're sick and back here in the hospital."

"Well, I hope I DO see you again. Like somewhere outside the hospital when we're done being sick."

"I like that better." She smiled, turned around, and walked into her room. The next morning, I went home.

Thursday, November 17, 1983

Sometime around lunch, I felt a canker sore in my mouth, right in the middle of my right cheek. By dinner, I had about four more, three on the sides of my tongue. It hurt. It hurt a lot! I didn't want to eat dinner. I couldn't eat dinner.

Mom said, "Here, try to eat this." She gave me a Dixie cup of ice cream, half chocolate, half vanilla. "You have to eat something." Then she turned to my dad and yelled, "Go get the prescription!"

I guess my feeding tube was feeling neglected and this was its way of shouting, "Now it's my time!" The chemo that caused mouth sores was kicking in. The doctors had given my parents a prescription for a medicine that I was supposed to rinse with when my mouth sores got bad. The sores were getting bad. It felt like if I opened my mouth, the sores would stretch and bleed. I sucked the ice cream off the little wooden spoon through my teeth. The coldness soothed the sores for a brief moment, but it was temporary relief. In fact, once I swallowed the ice cream, the sores hurt even more. It was a terrible quandary. Was the temporary relief worth the sores hurting even more afterward? I just wanted to go to sleep so I wouldn't have to make this agonizing decision.

Finally, Dad showed up with a huge bottle of medicine. We poured a tablespoon into a cup. It was yellow—deep, thick yellow—and it smelled terrible. It smelled like Robitussin if they had it in potato flavor.

"Rinse your mouth with this. It's supposed to soothe your mouth," Dad urged.

I took a swig and rinsed. The rinsing hurt. It put pressure on the sores, which just amplified the pain.

Reading off the bottle, Dad said, "Rinse for at least thirty seconds. Then repeat as necessary up to three times an hour."

I held the liquid in my mouth for an excruciating 30 seconds. My eyes were tearing and then overflowing; the overflow of tears dripped down my cheeks. Finally, I spit out into the sink.

"Does that help?" Mom asked.

I shook my head. I couldn't even open my mouth to say the word.

"Do it again," Dad directed. I did it again. And again. And again. And again. And one last time. Six times, double the allotted amount, and still no relief. I stood up and walked, almost in a frenzy, around the kitchen and living room, mindlessly searching for something to distract me. My parents came up behind me. They both held me, and I started to cry. The cry became a sob that quickly morphed into a weep. The three of us collapsed onto the floor,

Dad holding me tight, rocking me, and Mom stroking my phantom hair. From my peripheral, I could see my brothers at the top of the stairs, watching. Evan and I locked eyes for a moment, then he walked away into his room and blasted an album. Jeremy followed him.

Twenty minutes later, the pain finally started to subside. My parents and I sat up and looked at each other.

"I think it's time we open up that tube and feed you," Dad suggested.

Mom took out one of the hundreds of nutritional shakes that the hospital had given us. Actually, they had *given* us only a one-month supply. We happened to come into possession of an extra six-month supply. Our neighbor Ben is somehow involved, but that's all I know.

I took my shirt off. I loosened the head of the gastrostomy tube from my bare body. I popped open the shake. Dad inserted a small plastic funnel into the opening. Mom slowly poured the shake in. We all sat and watched. And waited.

"Do you feel anything?" Dad asked, genuinely curious.

"Umm, it feels cold? I think?" I answered. It did feel cold. The shake went through the tube and directly into my stomach. I felt something, but it's hard to describe. Maybe like an ice cream brain freeze without the throbbing pain. My skin wasn't cold, but the shake was cold on the inside of my stomach.

"Do you want more? How do you know when you're full?" Mom asked just as curiously as Dad.

"How am I supposed to know?" I answered just as curiously as my parents. "I guess give me whatever they say is one serving." So that's what they did. And I think I felt a little full.

I woke up at about 5:00 A.M. with my mouth burning so much that it made the previous episode seem like a campfire compared to the inferno I now felt. I ran to the bathroom, crying, and started rinsing with the yellow goop.

After three rinses, Dad came in and stopped me. "Only three rinses. Only three." I looked up at him, my cheeks flushed, my eyes pleading for help. There was nothing he could do, nothing anyone could do. I just had to endure it. Dad picked me up and, after a moment of hesitation, brought me to the same spot on the living room floor where the earlier episode had played out. I was wailing, but I couldn't open my mouth. It came out as a stifled scream/sniffle as snot and tears and spit came out my eyes and nose. I imagine the sound and stuff coming out was similar to being tortured while having your mouth duct-taped shut.

Dad held me and rocked me for the 20 minutes it took for the pain to subside. For the next three months or so, this became a daily—sometimes twice daily—routine, with certain variations. Sometimes Dad would be at work so Mom would rock me.

If it wasn't too bad, I would rock myself in the fetal position, trying to get through it. I started counting things during my episodes. I counted cracks in the ceiling. I counted table legs or stains on the lime-green living room carpet. Whatever was in my line of sight. Over and over. I'd count the number of items sitting on the desk. I'd count the stairs and picture myself walking up and down them over and over again, counting each step. This became my coping mechanism. It was my way of focusing on something other than the pain in my mouth.

When you're a kid, you really have no idea how much your parents love you. One night, after a particularly bad, almost vomit-inducing episode with my mouth sores, I was lying in bed with my parents. I was almost asleep. Mom said something like, "If I could take your place…"

Then I heard Dad say, "You know we're doing everything we can for you, kid. I'd throw myself in front of a train if it would take away your pain."

"But you'd die," I managed to whisper. Dad just smiled. Big and genuine, as if the thought of him being able to do that was the greatest thing ever. That was powerful. That smile said more to me than any words could ever dare try to say.

Thursday, December 1, 1983

Interesting week. Saturday is my birthday. I'll be turning 13. I'm not sure if I feel 13. I know I don't look 13—especially wearing these hats that my Aunt Mari from Chicago knitted and sent to me. They aren't even hats. I guess you can call them skullcaps. They are basically yarn that hugs my bald head. And she made them in fluorescent colors. They wouldn't be so bad if she had knitted a Yankees logo or something cool on them. Instead, I am wearing bright yellow, bright pink, and lime green hats. Some even have a splash of purple in them. I shouldn't complain, though. When you're bald and it is wintertime, you find out real quickly that heat leaves your body through your head. And as silly as these hats make me look, they definitely keep me warm. So I'm turning 13 and look like an eight-year-old girl.

Saturday, my 13th birthday, was also supposed to be my bar mitzvah, which had to be canceled. We have about 60 plastic, coin-sorting Yankees banks that we had been planning to give out as favors. They're sitting in boxes in our living room, taunting me, mocking me. Yesterday, I took one into the garage and smashed it with an aluminum bat—just beat the piss out of it. It felt good. Made me smile. I think I might do that again, often.

I discovered two gross things about my feeding tube. One is that if I don't wash the base of the tube adjacent to my skin after each feeding, some stomach juice backs up and cakes onto my skin. After a few hours, it hardens and starts to smell. Then my mom and I have to carefully peel it off the tube and off my skin. It is very gross. I imagine it's how barnacles attach to docks in a marina and have to be peeled off with ice picks—only my barnacles are crust made from stomach juice.

The other gross thing is actually cooler than gross, although it is still kind of gross. When I have the stopper off my feeding tube and put the funnel in, I can reverse the flow of what is in my stomach using my stomach muscles. If I clench my abs, any liquid that is in my stomach, and that includes chunks of partially digested food, backs up into the funnel and I can look at it. If I keep my abs clenched, I can pool a few ounces in the funnel for about 30 seconds. I can watch food particles floating around like tadpoles. It is my own personal food aquarium. It's gross, I know, but I find it really interesting.

Evan got his report card. He failed three classes. That's very un-Evan like. He's always been a straight-A student. He's also always been very school spirited. In fact, I think he was voted Most School Spirited in his 8th grade yearbook. This year, his sophomore year, he is the class president, so failing a class is an event for him. Failing three classes is catastrophic.

It is also catastrophic for my dad. Dad, although funny and sarcastic, is very strict about a few things—grades, chores, and not taking advantage of Mom, which three boys can very easily do. With grades, it's not that he'll kill us if we don't get straight A's but more that he expects us to work our hardest and do better than the best we can. Incidentally, all three of us are very good students and very capable of straight A's, so actually, he pretty much kills us when we don't get them.

Needless to say, Evan and Dad had a few words when that report card came home.

After dinner, of which I was only able to eat apple-sauce, while Evan was doing the dishes and I was not really helping him, he confronted me. With no warning, he turned directly to me and said, "I get it, Tim. I really get it. I get that you're sick and you need extra attention from Mom and Dad. And I get that it's not your fault. I'm not blaming anything on you. But this is a family of five, not three. Jeremy and me are affected by you, too."

"Where is this coming from? What are you talking about?"

"Let me fill you in on life for the rest of us outside of Cancer World. Since you've been sick, I'm failing three classes in school. Jeremy is lost. He's starting to ask questions, real questions about you that I don't want to have to answer. I'm like his surrogate parent, but I don't want that! I'd tell him to ask Mom, but she's always with you. And Jeremy and I, well, Jeremy..." He paused here as though he was embarrassed to admit it. "We need Mom and Dad, too."

"Maybe you should be talking with Mom and Dad about this, not me."

"Maybe you should try to be a little less needy. Be a little more self-sufficient."

I was mad and hurt. Screw him. "Screw you, you jerk! You don't think I'd rather be back to normal?" Then I raised my voice real loud, something I'd never even come close to doing before, and yelled at him, "WHAT DO YOU WANT ME TO DO?"

With barely a pause, he replied very matter-of-factly, "Go away. I like it better when you're in the hospital."

I almost started to cry from anger and shock. I left the room and heard Evan throw what sounded like an extremely wet sponge against the wall.

Of course a few hours later, I had a terrible mouth-sore episode, which is when I am at my neediest. It was about 8:00 P.M. Dad was out picking up Evan and a buddy at the mall. Jeremy was in his bed, waiting to be tucked in, and I was rinsing my mouth vigorously in the bathroom. Evan's mini-tirade had pissed me off, but it had also gotten me thinking. Maybe I should try to endure some of this myself. Unfortunately, this episode was too much to bear. I ran into my mom's room, where she was folding laundry. I just looked at her, tears streaming down my face, and she knew. She brought me to her bed and cradled my head in her lap, rocking me slowly, rubbing my back.

Jeremy, ready to be tucked into bed, yelled, "Mom! I'm ready!"

"Give me a few minutes! I'll be right there!" Mom yelled back. Jeremy's room was adjacent to my parents' room. A minute passed.

"Mom! I'm ready!" Jeremy yelled again.

"Just wait!" Mom snapped back. "Timmy needs me!"

That must have been the trigger for Jeremy. For the next 10 minutes, we got his version of Evan's sentiment. "Sick boy needs his mommy!" he yelled mockingly. "Sick boy! Sick boy is mommy's favorite! Stupid sick boy!" I looked up at my mom and, with my eyes, pleaded for her to leave me and go to him.

"No, I'll deal with him later." She held me tighter. I have to admit that earlier, I had thought Evan was being a selfish jerk. But hearing this venom come out of Jeremy confirmed that they really were having difficulty with this. They hated me!

"Sick boy! Sick boy! Stupid sick boy mouth!"

Mom laughed at that one. And as Jeremy continued his "sick boy" rant, he started running out of things to yell. It started to sound silly, and Mom laughed at each one.

"Stupid sick boy! Why don't you go crying to your mommy! Oh, wait...you ALREADY ARE!"

A few more minutes passed, and as my mouth pain started to ease, I started laughing with Mom. We heard a good three minutes of silence, and we assumed that Jeremy was done.

Then, feebly, with hardly any venom left, he said, "I hate sick boy."

I looked up at Mom.

She rolled her eyes and said, "He doesn't mean it. He just misses me. And he misses you, too." Then she left to tuck him in.

A half hour later, with Jeremy asleep, Mom went to get me some "food" for my tube. Dad and Evan walked in the house.

"Feeding time?" Dad asked, as if I were a pet hamster.

"Yep," I said. I didn't look at Evan.

A moment passed. Evan broke the awkward silence. "You want an appetizer?" He tossed an M&M into the funnel. It rolled around, settled into the hole, and went down the tube. "How'd it taste?" Evan asked, half-smiling.

"Is that bad for me?"

"I don't know," said Dad. "I don't see why it would be. We'll be right back." He and Evan left the room and came back in two minutes with a bunch of goodies. They started throwing things in the funnel like a carnival game—Rice Krispies, Skittles, miniature marshmallows. Evan even poured some Fun Dip down the tube. We were all laughing and having a good time. There was no evidence of the argument Evan and I had had earlier.

Finally, Evan suggested, "How about you top it off with a beer?"

"Oh, right, smart guy," Dad said as he playfully got Evan in a headlock and tousled his hair. "He's had enough snacks. He'll be drunk off all that sugar!"

As Dad and Evan left the room, Evan turned back and we locked eyes and did the same goofy half-smile at each other.

Friday, December 2, 1983

I got two letters from Tess. One was a birthday card. The other was six and a half pages of real personal stuff. She wrote all about her family and friends back home. She wrote that she had told her best friend in Iowa about me and that she and I were a couple. She even had a nickname for us, Dynamite. "You know," she wrote, "Timmy-n-Tess, TNT."

She wrote about how much she liked hanging out with me and that she really hoped we could see each other again on healthier terms. That warmed me. Made me feel real good.

Then she got into how she hasn't been feeling well the past three weeks. She even missed a Bingo night. She was trying not to get depressed but notices it creeping out. She snaps at her mom or, worse, ignores her. She thinks it'll pass. The doctors are worried about her white blood cells and they're talking about moving her to isolation. No decisions have been made. She is hoping it won't come to that.

Lastly, she sent me a picture of her, pre-cancer. In the picture, Tess is wearing a gray hooded sweatshirt with a dark-blue down vest over it. She has on jeans, but not designer jeans like Sassoon or Jordache. Tess is sitting on a wooden fence with horses in the background. Her hair is long, straight, and light brown. She has cute bangs that stop just above her eyebrows. Her hair is in a ponytail and pulled to her left side, lying over her left shoulder. Her eyebrows are mocha brown and kind of thick. She has the same big toothy smile, but her lips are redder—not from lipstick, but from healthiness. Of course, in the picture, her blue eyes are amplified by long, dark eyelashes. And they're big and wide, as if amazing stories were constantly being told in her ear. She is gorgeous and cute and, dare I say, hot! I immediately kissed the picture, recognized that that was a silly 11-year-old girl thing to do, didn't care, and did it again.

Then I went searching for a picture of me to send to her. I picked one of me playing baseball, of course. I had my uniform on and my bat resting up on my shoulder like a rifle. I purposefully picked a picture with my cap off so she could see my hair. I thought that was important.

I reread her letter two more times, and it reminded me of a book I had read in 5th grade called *The Big Wave* by Pearl S. Buck. The book is about a Japanese village that lies between the ocean and a volcano. A tidal wave (the BIG WAVE!) comes and wipes out the fishermen living on the beach. One character, a boy, survives and goes to live with his friend's family up on the mountain. The book goes on to tell about how the boy and his new family cope and move on with their lives. The main theme is "life is stronger than death." We are all going to die; that's a fact. But if we live in fear of that moment, we cannot live a happy life—and what kind of life is that? We must focus on living, not spend our time worrying about dying.

I wrote about that in my letter back to Tess. Then I told her more about my brothers and my school and my friends. I put the letter and my picture in an envelope. I gave it to Mom to mail, and then I went upstairs and reread *The Big Wave*.

Saturday, December 3, 1983

Today's my birthday. I'm 13. I went to the bathroom, stood in my underwear in front of the mirror, and made a mental note of how not 13 I looked. Completely hairless, slightly hunched over, still prepubescent, with a thin white tube hanging from my chest and a thicker yellow tube protruding from my stomach. I looked pathetic. It is unbelievable to me that a girl as pretty as Stephanie had been so eager to make out with me just two months ago. Man, it seems like a lifetime ago.

Mike and Victoria came over after lunch to say hi and to give birthday wishes. I'm starting to suspect that they might be into each other. I hate to be selfish, but I hope they aren't.

They walked in, and I immediately realized that I hadn't put my wig on. In front of my family or Mike, I didn't care, but with Victoria here, I felt very self-conscious. But I had nothing to worry about. She didn't even flinch when she saw me. I mean, maybe she was puking her guts out in her head, but on the outside, she didn't give any inkling that she thought I was gross.

After a while of catching up on gossip, Mike telling me about all his detentions, and us guys talking sports about which Victoria couldn't care less but kindly endured, talk turned to the 8th grade dance.

Mike blurted, "I think I'm going to ask Melissa to the dance. Her and Andy Sacks broke up. And I hear she loves to make out. Plus, she's got nice boobs!"

Victoria smiled, blushed, and self-consciously crossed her arms even though she was dressed very conservatively. Then she said, "It's six months away. You'll probably change your mind at least three times."

"At least three HUNDRED times," I chimed in.

"Yeah, I guess. Plus, ya never know what can happen on the Washington trip," Mike said.

"Thanks for depressing me. You know I can't go."

"So what? I can't talk about it? That's stupid."

Victoria interrupted. "Maybe you'll be better by then."

"I still have a year of chemo. I don't think so."

"But maybe the doctors will let you go to the dance," she continued.

"Interesting that you are so eager to talk about the dance, isn't it, Victoria? My dear lady, why don't you tell Timbo what you told me earlier?"

Victoria shot Mike a dirty look. Then she said, "Well, I was just thinking that if you can go, I want to go with you."

"Really?" I think the color ran back into my pale skin. "You want *me* to be your date? Have you seen me lately?"

"It's not about that. And it's not charity. It'd be fun, is all. If you can go."

I smiled big. Couldn't help it. Mike puckered his lips and smooched the air, mocking me behind Victoria's back. If she hadn't been looking directly at me, I'd have given him the finger.

"Alright, Victoria. I'm in. Thanks. You're right. It'd be fun."

Later, after dinner, I opened my presents. There were a lot of them. Many were from relatives I'd never gotten presents from before. Some were from people I didn't even know existed, like people from the town and people my dad worked with. The PTA of my elementary school gave me a $200 check, the money coming from a bake sale they had done in my honor. I picked up my last present. It was a tiny envelope, maybe 2" x 2". On the front it said "Tim" in big red-marker letters. I immediately knew it was from Jeremy. As I opened the envelope, Jeremy got up and walked out of the room. I took out a plain white card. On the front, it said the same sentence over and over again, about 10 times:

I hope you feel better.
I hope you feel better.
I hope you feel better.
I hope you feel better.
I hope you feel better.
I hope you feel better.
I hope you feel better.
I hope you feel better.
I hope you feel better.
I hope you feel better.

I opened the card, and on the inside it said the same thing about 20 more times. "I hope you feel better." And on the back, eight more. At the bottom, it simply said, "Jeremy." I felt myself start to tear up (when had I become such a wimp?!?), and I left the room. I saw Jeremy sitting on the stairs, and I sat next to him.

I leaned in and quietly said, "I'm sorry."

He tilted his head up to me, smiled awkwardly, and said, "I hope you feel better."

"Right now, Jeremy, I do." Then I took his card and put it next to Tess's picture. And every morning, those are the first two things that I look at to start my day.

Thursday, December 22, 1983

It was my 25th and last radiation treatment. We arrived at the hospital, I got into the wheelchair in the lobby, and the orderly pushed me into the elevator. **Second floor – Radiology.**

The elevator opened on the second floor. Normally, when the doors opened, I got a little bummed, knowing that I had to get a treatment. The real bad part of the radiation experience was the smell that permeated my nose for the 10 to 15 seconds the treatment took. It's nauseating. And during some treatments, it was a major struggle to hold down my vomit.

Similar to how I had begun counting things to help me deal with pain, I had made up routines to get me through my radiation treatments. Today, though, I was giddy—ecstatic, even—knowing it was going to be the last time I'd be cramped in that terrible mask, so I went through my coping routine smiling, almost singing my way through it.

The first sign I see in the hallway says, **GASTROEN-TEROLOGY,** and each day, I sing it to myself as if saying, "nanny-nanny-poo-poo." Around the first corner, I always slap the two-toned wall—the light brown top half first and the grape-green bottom half second. Today, because I was so happy, I drummed the wall instead of giving it one slap. Then I realized I had broken my routine. On the last day!!! That's a jinx! So then I made sure I did the rest of the routine perfectly. I counted the hallway beds (four today), I dragged my toes on the floor for 15 seconds, and when we arrived at the radiation suite, I traced my hands three times around the wheels of the wheelchair. Then I prayed the radiation gods hadn't noticed my inadvertent drumming, the same way Charlie and Grandpa had hoped Willy Wonka hadn't noticed that they'd drunk the bubble liquid that made them fly.

Do you remember that movie? Willy Wonka *did* notice, and Charlie and Grandpa got reamed out and almost lost the contest. My fate was similar. The radiation gods *did* notice my break in the routine, and on my final day of radiation, I puked five seconds into my treatment. Being trapped in the mask, I couldn't turn my head, and the puke dribbled out of my mouth and nose. My eyes teared, and my cheeks filled with vomit. I was gagging and trying not to choke on it. Nobody came in to unstrap me for what was an eternal 10 seconds. Finally, the technicians came running in, unstrapped my head, and turned me on my side, and I let it all out. I think I heard one of the technicians gag and dry heave. It was that messy.

I was afraid that I'd have to do it over—that because I had yakked, the treatment wouldn't count or had made them miss the mark. But like Charlie and Grandpa, who ultimately won, after a three-minute conference between the technicians and a doctor, it was determined that I was free. No more radiation! That was a milestone!

Now all I had to endure was 13 more months of chemotherapy.

"One thing at a time, Tim," Mom said after I was all cleaned up. "Baby steps."

Wednesday, December 28, 1983.

I got a holiday card from Tess. It was just a picture of her with Jack the Clown in the teen room. In her left hand was a copy of the book *The Big Wave*. In the picture, she and Jack are waving and smiling. She signed it "Happy New Year, Tim! It WILL be a happy one, for BOTH of us! xoxoxoxoxo Tess."

Tuesday, April 3, 1984

Overall, the past three months have been good ones. The mouth sores have pretty much stopped being so terrible. I get a bad one maybe once a week, but the bad ones now are tolerable. I pretty much eat normally, but my capacity to open my mouth has diminished greatly. At best, I can open my mouth wide enough to just fit a small hotdog in. No bun, though. Because of that, I still prefer a liquid diet or a tube feeding, but my doctors say I have to start chewing real food again.

Last month, our neighbor Ben came through on wrestling night. My dad, my brothers, and I got to sit on the front-row at a professional wrestling match. It was awesome! All the stars were there! The best part was that after the match, we got to go backstage and meet the Iron Sheik, Tito Santana, Bob Backlund, that new guy named Hulk Hogan (who is huge, but I still don't think he is going to be that good), and my favorite, Jimmy "Superfly" Snuka. They all signed a faux championship belt for me. I've since put the belt on display in our living room. It was a great night.

On the way home, in the car, Jeremy said, "Maybe you should stay sick. That was awesome!"

Last week, I had to go into the hospital for two inpatient days. It wasn't my white blood cells the doctors were worried about this time. It was my platelets. I needed a blood transfusion.

About 25 minutes after Mom and I arrived on the fifth floor, I had an IV in my arm and I was sitting in a recliner in a room with about seven other kids, their moms, and a large TV on the wall. Letting someone else's blood drip into my body one drop at a time is a long, boring five-hour process.

At one point, a doctor I'd never seen before came into the room and corralled all the moms into the hallway. He spoke with them for about 10 minutes and handed them each a pamphlet.

"What's that?" I asked when Mom came back in.

"It's nothing. Watch your TV," Mom answered, blowing off my question. I decided not to pursue it—at least not right then.

Later that night, my brothers and I were playing Adventure on our Atari 2600, which we had bought with the PTA check from the fundraiser from my elementary school that was supposed to help us pay medical bills (shh…don't tell anybody) when Mom and Dad called me into the kitchen.

"Here, look at this." Dad tossed me the pamphlet that Mom had gotten at the hospital. I looked at it. At the top was a huge yellow smiley face splitting the two-word title:

CAMP SUNSHINE

Underneath the title was a collage of a couple dozen kids at a summer camp doing various activities: swimming, archery, canoeing, soccer, and arts and crafts. A few kids had their arms around each other, smiling at the camera. All of the kids were bald. All of them.

"What's this?" I asked dubiously.

Dad answered, "It's a camp that is sponsored by the hospital. It's a three-week program, and it's for kids that have cancer."

"And you're showing me this why?"

"Because you can go if you want," Dad answered.

"It looks fun!" Mom tried to sound enthusiastic. "You might like it. It's a sleep-away camp."

"Don't you mean YOU might like it? A three-week break from me?"

"Hey! Don't talk to your mom like that! That's not what this is about. We just thought it's something you might be interested in, since you can't go to Camp Keewee this summer."

"Ooh, maybe you'll get to second base with a bald chick." Evan had entered the room and seemed to be enjoying this.

Dad ignored him. "Look, it's just something you should consider. Your mom's right. It actually looks fun. And you'll be around other kids in the same situation as you."

It hit me at that moment that I wouldn't be going to Camp Keewee this summer. That'd been our camp for the past six years. I had known I'd be missing all of 8th grade, the Washington, DC, trip, and probably the dance, but camp was so far away that it hadn't even occurred to me that missing camp was a possibility. Now, that reality hit me. I didn't know how to react or what to say. I had no desire to spend my summer with other sick kids. I wanted to spend my summer with MY friends. In normal camp. Especially considering the way last summer had ended with the Alley-Oop party. This summer, I was hoping to raise the bar.

"Think about it," Mom suggested.

"Is Tess going?" I asked.

Mom looked at me and gave me a weak smile. "I called her mom, and Tess isn't going. She's not healthy enough. But you should still consider it. Really, Timmy, it might be good for you."

"Alright, I'll think about it." But I already knew my answer. There was no way I was going.

Generally, my routine for the past three months and for the near future was that every other week, I'd go to Sloan for outpatient chemo, which, unfortunately, included a Vincristine day. I wasn't allowed to go see Tess when I was an outpatient, and she wasn't allowed to come over and see me. Too much risk of infection. But every time I was at Sloan, I had a nurse take Tess a letter I had written or a small gift. Usually, the nurse brought me notes back from Tess. I loved reading her notes. They're funny, silly, romantically corny, and sometimes serious. Lately, Tess has been getting very philosophical in her notes. I got this tidbit in one of her recent notes: "Quadriplegics envy paraplegics. They think they've got it made." After that, she wrote, "It's all about perspective." She's a smart kid, that Tess. She should be writing motivational posters. Another of my Tess favorites: "Fear is something you have to throw into a corner. Constantly. Because it never goes away."

But the best one, she got from an old yearbook that she had found on the street back in Iowa. The caption for a photo read, "Yesterday was the past, tomorrow is the future. But today is a gift. That's why it's called the present."

I wanted Tess to enjoy my notes as much as I enjoyed hers, so I tried to give her a few sayings. They were probably not as good, and they're sports-oriented, but I tried: "They say of a broken bat that yields a base hit…it died a hero." And I got one from a magazine: "If you want to be a champion, practice your weakness."

Thursday, April 26, 1984

I got my feeding tube taken out today. The mouth sores are gone, and I'm eating enough solid food to have gained a little weight. The doctors saw no reason why I needed the tube any longer.

Dad took the day off and went with me to the hospital. He kept joking that the doctors were just going to yank the tube out. I kept insisting that they were going to put me out first and then surgically remove it since, I might remind him, it was embedded into my stomach.

"Nope," Dad insisted. "They're just going to lay you down and yank it out."

We got to the hospital and were eventually put on the surgery ward.

"See," I said sarcastically to Dad.

"No, YOU'LL see," he returned smugly.

I put on another open-in-the-back gown, sat on the bed, and waited for an anesthesiologist to come in. Dad was just looking at me and smiling. A big know-it-all smile. Like he knew something I didn't. He was getting me nervous.

"Are they really going to just yank it out?"

Dad looked at me and nodded.

"I'm sure they're at least going to numb it," I said, mostly to convince myself.

Dad just shook his head. The doctor came in. He laid me back, lifted my gown, and examined the tube. He palpated the area around it and said, "I'll be right back."

"With the anesthesiologist, right?" I called after him, but he either ignored me or didn't hear me, because he didn't respond.

Five minutes later, the doctor came back. Solo. He reached under my gown, grabbed the tube almost at the base, slapped my belly hard, and YANKED the tube right out of me like he was pulling weeds.

"Wha…!" I was ready to scream, but I didn't feel any pain. A nurse came in and put a bandage over the hole. The doctor held the tube above me and asked, "You want it?"

"The tube?"

"Yeah. You want to keep it?"

"No."

"You sure?" Dad asked. "You could make a necklace out of it."

"No!"

The doctor continued, "Okay. Keep the hole bandaged for two days. It should heal nicely. You'll have a small scar, maybe a small indentation, but it'll look okay. Chicks dig scars." And he left. I looked at Dad, and he whistled nonchalantly. That son of a gun had been right. They yanked it right out of me.

Friday, June 8, 1984

The Washington, DC, trip was this past week. Mike came over to tell me all the juice. There was a scandalous hook-up on the trip. But he made me sweat it out.

"C'mon, Tim, guess."

"I have no idea. It could be anyone."

"Guess! You'll never guess it."

"Then why you making me guess? Just tell me!"

"Okay, it wasn't anyone we're tight with. It wasn't Stephanie. It wasn't anyone from the lunch group. It wasn't—"

"Seriously, dude. Enough. Who was it?"

"It was Mrs. Ortiz and Mr. Edwards."

"No way! Two teachers?"

"Yeah, man. Vinny Zamon snuck out of his room. He planned on going out and scamming some cigarettes at a deli around the corner from the hotel. He got to the lobby and sees Ortiz and Edwards having drinks at the hotel bar. Not a big deal, but, according to Vinny, she was drunk and hanging on him and touching him, and then he saw Edwards put his hand on her butt. Vinny—that guy's awesome—he watched them for about fifteen minutes. He said they were making out and they finally took the elevator upstairs together, her hand in his back pocket."

"That's phenomenal! Any fallout?"

"It gets better. The next day, Ortiz shows up for breakfast with a huge hickey on her neck. She tried to cover it, but everyone knew. Vinny had spread the word about what he saw."

"Did Vinny get in trouble?"

"Yeah, but he said it was worth it. Good trip ya missed, my man!" He slapped my leg.

"What about you and Melissa? Anything?"

Mike leaned back on the couch and put his feet up on the coffee table. "We made out a little. Not a big deal. I mean, it was fun and she's hot! I asked her to go to the dance next week. She said yes. I told her that we'd go and hang with you and Victoria, assuming you can go. Mel wants to hang with Vinny and those guys, but I told her I'm hanging with you."

"That's cool, Mike. But you don't have to babysit me, ya know. You wanna hang with those guys, that's okay. Really."

"Tim, we've been looking forward to this dance since sixth grade. We're going together. If Melissa doesn't want to hang, forget her." He paused. "In fact, she bailed on me this morning. So it's just you, Victoria, and me. I'll be your backup. If you can't go, I'll be Victoria's date. If you can go, I'll be both of your dates."

Friday, June 15, 1984

I got the go-ahead from the doctor on Monday about the dance. I called Victoria, and she seemed genuinely excited. I warned her that I couldn't go all out and that I understood if she wanted to go with someone else. She pooh-poohed me and said she'd meet at my house on Friday.

Getting dressed for the dance was a little depressing. I was feeling a little down and unworthy. I put on one of Evan's white T-shirts, big enough to comfortably fit over my broviac. I put on my suit shirt and tie. Then my pants. Then my wig. I've come to hate that wig. It looks terrible. It looks nothing even close to real hair anymore. And it's been stretched a little, so sometimes, if I get bumped, it turns a little. I should just go bald.

I looked in the mirror, and my pathetic reflection jumped out at me. I noticed my missing eyelashes and eyebrows, the dark discoloration on the sides of my face compared to the paleness of the front from the radiation. The paleness contrasted with my dark blue suit, which made my face look like a white onion. The suit seemed too big on me. It practically swallowed me. I put the wig on, fixed it the best I could, and, after a good seven minutes, decided that, at the moment, the wig was the lesser of two evils. Better fake hair than no hair.

Victoria arrived on time with her parents, her older sister, and her younger sister. Our families could be the Brady bunch, with me and Victoria playing Peter and Jan. Our dads shook hands, our moms hugged, our older siblings—both sophomores—talked school, and our younger siblings sat around, anxiously waiting for something to happen.

I saw Victoria come walking up the driveway. She looked amazing all dressed up. That was expected, but what I hadn't expected was how much older she looked. She really looked like a young adult, like she'd fit right in with high school girls, whereas I looked and felt like I'd fit in with Jeremy's 4th grade class.

Victoria wore her hair straight down to the middle of her back, with two skinny braids hanging off each side of her face. A white flower clip held her hair off her face. She wore a light blue dress with puffy shoulders that was cut low in the front and back. In the back, her hair covered what her dress did not. In the front, a necklace accented what her dress did not cover. It was very difficult not to stare at her chest—which, by the way, had gotten noticeably larger. When did that happen? Victoria was wearing high heels, which made her about five or six inches taller than me, which made my line of sight right between her neck and her boobs. This was going to be awkwardly interesting.

"Wow, Victoria," I said. "You look...fabulous."

She blushed. "Thanks. I'm so glad we're doing this." She leaned down and kissed my cheek. Jeremy and Victoria's younger sister giggled, and Victoria blushed again.

We stood and posed for pictures. It was hard for me to get over the fact that Victoria looked more like my older sister or my aunt than like my friend/date. Mike and his mom showed up, and Mike ran up to us to get into a few pictures.

After 15 more minutes of pictures and pleasantries, Mike, Victoria, and I all piled into the backseat of our car, my dad being the driver. On the way, my dad was surprisingly quiet, no jokes. I think he was more content to listen to our conversation.

"I'm not gonna lie to you guys," I said. "I'm nervous. I haven't seen most of these people in eight months."

Mike jumped in. "Don't sweat it. They're your friends. You were popular, remember? Everyone liked you. They still will. They may not know how to react to you, but they'll be cool."

Victoria added sweetly, "Tim, they're looking forward to seeing you. They WANT to see you. They all miss you, ya know."

When we arrived, Dad said, "Have fun, guys. I'll pick you up at eleven-thirty. If there's a problem—" He looked at Victoria and Mike. "Call me. Understand?"

"Yes, sir," they both answered.

We stepped out, and I hesitated. Mike noticed and mouthed, "You can do it."

Mike took charge and led the way as Victoria and I walked a few steps behind. Everyone was looking. I heard a lot of "Hey, Tim! Glad you can make it! It's so good to see you!" But all these good wishes were said from a distance, as if they were afraid to come too close to me. I was okay with that. I think.

As we made our way through the crowd of people, I became a little oblivious to what people were saying because I couldn't get over how everyone looked. They ALL looked so much bigger and older. I was always small, but I assumed I'd catch up and not be the runt of the 8th grade litter. The guys were massive compared to me. A few shook my hand and patted me on the back, and it made me feel fragile. Their hands easily dwarfed mine. Some sported facial hair. But the biggest difference between eight months before and now was mostly in their chests and biceps and voices. They weren't kids anymore. They were young men. They had biceps that seemed capable of manly things. Some of the guys were slapping each other playfully on the chest, and it sounded like armor.

And the girls! I used to barely notice them. They practically weren't there. Not in any way that interested me, anyway. Now, I couldn't miss them. They were all over the place. I used to just think of them as being someone's annoying sisters, or they weren't on my radar at all. Now it's like all I could think about is how I wanted to... I wasn't sure I even knew exactly, but I knew it was something. All these girls I'd known since kindergarten as bike-riding buddies and silly little annoyances had all become interesting—disturbing, even. All of a sudden, they all clearly had breasts that they covered with folded arms, which ironically drew even more attention to them. And the girls smelled good, too.

Then I looked at Mike joking around with his/our buddies, and at Victoria with her girlfriends fixing each other's hair and lifting each other's dresses as they giggled, and I was flabbergasted. Mike and Victoria, too, had made the leap into the world of young adulthood, a world I was far removed from. I never realized Mike and Victoria were living in this new habitat.

Despite everyone being so nice and starting to come up to me, it all made me feel very lonely.

Mike, Victoria, and I settled in at a table with three other couples, and immediately, Mike was up and dancing. He danced by himself, with random girls, with other guys. He was having a blast. And he is a terrible dancer. But he has no shame. I heard people laughing at his bad dancing, and I thought, *At least he's out there. He's not hiding on the sidelines,* talking *about dancing, secretly wishing he were dancing but not having the nerve to do it.* He was dancing! He just put himself out there, not aware, not caring, what others thought. I found that admirable.

"Victoria, if you don't mind, I'll be right back." I maneuvered my way onto the dance floor toward Mike. I sensed people watching me, waiting to see what was going to happen.

Mike saw me, grabbed my hand, and playfully twirled me like a girl, back and forth a few times. I was laughing. He was laughing and playing it up. At one point, I felt a little dizzy and told him to slow down just a little, and he did. But we were hamming it up. And I felt alive. I felt like I belonged.

Victoria came up next to me and bumped my hip. She smiled, and we did an easy step-clap while Mike went through his funky routine as "Sunglasses at Night" blared from the DJ table. Slowly, others came up around us, and by the end of the song, we had a group of people dancing in a big circle, and I felt genuinely happy.

Prince's "When Doves Cry" came on, and I whispered to Victoria, "I'm okay. Just a little tired. I'm gonna sit for a few."

"You sure? You want me to come with you?"

"No, I want you to stay and dance and have fun. I'm really okay."

I walked away smiling. I made it back to my seat, sat down, and watched my friends have a good time. I was very happy with myself—a complete 180-degree turn from earlier when I had been looking pathetically at myself in the mirror.

Mr. Villone was chaperoning the dance. He came over and sat next to me. We talked sports and had the obligatory, "How are you feeling?" conversation.

Then he said to me, "Look, baseball, unfortunately, has to be put on hold. It's unfortunate, but that's what it is. But you should stay in the loop, try to stay active. I told Mr. Robinson to find you next year, but you should find him. He's a science teacher at the high school, but he's also the bowling coach. If you can, join the bowling team. If nothing else, it'll keep your arm in shape and your competitive spirit alive."

I thanked Mr. Villone. I like bowling. That wasn't a bad idea. I was contemplating the bowling-team thing when Mike came over to the table, dragging Stephanie along with him. They sat, and she said, "Hey, Tim. Good to see you."

"You, too, Steph."

Mike interrupted. "Okay, good. You guys good? No hard feelings?" We both rolled our eyes.

"Of course not," she said, smiling.

"Good," Mike continued. He gave Stephanie a little push, and she left the table. "You don't mind if Stephanie and I, ya know, hung out?"

"You wanna date Stéphanie?" He nodded to me. "She's all yours, bro. It's the least I could do."

"No, the least you could have done was not be such a good kisser. She says you kissed great. How do I live up to that?"

We laughed, and he jumped back on the dance floor. Victoria came over and sat, and we talked for a while, every so often interrupted by someone saying it was great to see me. It turns out that Victoria and I have a lot in common. I mean, she hates sports, doesn't know the difference between a touchdown and a home run. But we like the same music, books, and movies. She is just so easy to talk with. I never have to search for something to say.

As we were talking, "Straight from the Heart" by Bryan Adams came on. We both looked at each other and said, "I love this song." I stood up, took her hand, and led her to the dance floor, and we started to slow dance. I was looking up at her, my arms around her waist and her arms resting on my shoulders, hands clasped behind my neck. After a moment, she kicked off her heels to establish a more level eye line. To my right, I saw Mike slow-dancing with Stephanie. He gave me a thumbs-up behind her back.

At the end of the night, Mike, Stephanie, Victoria, and I sat on the curb outside the school, waiting for my dad to pick us up. Mike had his arm around Stephanie, and she was falling asleep on him. Her mom pulled up, they squeezed hands, and she got in the car.

"A good night, guys. A damn good night." He got up and walked away.

I turned to Victoria and said, "Thanks, Victoria. I had such a good time, and I wouldn't have come if you didn't ask. Thank you. And I really, um, I liked hanging with you and talking with you. You're an awesome girl."

"Tim, this was so much fun. You're an awesome guy."

There was a not-at-all awkward silence. There are probably a million better words to describe the moment, but the one that says it best is "nice." It was a nice moment.

"You know, I'm leaving for sleep-away camp in two weeks. I'll be gone until late August."

"Oh, that sounds like fun," I said, trying not to sound disappointed.

She smiled. "Before your dad comes, I want to give you this." She leaned in and kissed me, half on the cheek and half on the lips. It was a great kiss, and a special moment for me.

After Dad dropped Mike and Victoria off, I thought about the kiss. Besides making me miss Victoria already, it made me think about Tess.

Sunday, July 8, 1984

Summer is lonely. Mike is at a football camp in New Jersey. Victoria is at sleep-away camp. Jeremy and Evan go to Camp Keewee every day. I really miss my camp friends, but I'm glad that they won't see me the way I am right now—pale, small, with a wig, and all the other stuff. Most of them, I haven't seen since last summer. I certainly didn't want to see anyone from the Alley-Oop party. That would have been devastating.

I both dreaded and looked forward to dinner every evening so I could hear about what was going on at camp. Jeremy would talk about all the sports—whether or not we beat other camps in softball, soccer, basketball, etc., and who had done all the scoring. Evan would tell me about other types of scoring. He'd tell me all the gossip: who was hooking up with whom, who looked good, who looked not-so-good. I loved hearing it, but I hated not being a part of it, because I know I would have been a big player in both the sports and the gossip this summer.

Tomorrow, I start getting tutored. The guidance counselor at the high school came by our house for a visit.

My parents had spoken with him and told him all about my condition, and then he and I had talked briefly. He had told us that, as unfortunate as it may sound, I would have to get tutored this summer and pass the 8th grade finals if I wanted to continue with my class and move on to 9th grade—the alternative being to do 8th grade over. There was no debate, and starting tomorrow, from 8:30 to 11:30, Monday through Friday, I will be doing schoolwork. In the summer. Joy!

I got a letter from Tess's mom a few days ago. It basically said that Tess has not been feeling well at all. Tess keeps talking about me, and Tess's mom wants to know if I can come and visit. Soon.

I showed the letter to my mom, and on Wednesday afternoon, we're going into the city to see Tess.

Wednesday, July 11, 1984

We left after tutoring, at about 1:00 P.M., and got to Sloan at 2:30. I wanted to bring Tess a gift, but I had no idea what to get. At the last second, I bought her a bouquet of flowers on the street outside the hospital.

Mom and I walked into Tess's hospital room, and I immediately felt silly bringing her flowers. It seemed too contrived and too serious, so I left them outside the door. Tess was sitting in a chair by the window, hugging her knees up into her chest. She wore a long, barely pink head scarf that flowed down over her hospital gown, almost to the floor. Her head lolled to the right, resting on a pillow against the windowsill.

She looked at me, smiled, and asked, "Where are the flowers?"

"How did you know I brought flowers?"

"I saw you on the street from my window. Here, look."

I walked behind Tess and looked out the window. Sure enough, I could see the vendor I had bought the flowers from.

"I left them outside your door. I had second thoughts."

"I like flowers. I am a girl, ya know. I know I don't look it, but I am."

I didn't answer back. I just went to the door and got the flowers. As I walked back into the room, Tess's mom, Clara, said, "We'll go for a walk and leave you two alone for a while."

"But, Ma! I'm not even wearing a bra! Are you sure?" Tess snapped back uncharacteristically.

"Tess!" her mom shouted. Then, more calmly, as though she'd been through this before, she said, "We'll be back."

The moms left, and Tess said, "I'm sorry. Sometimes I can't help it. It's like I have this anger in me and I can only let it out with my mom. Then I feel terrible right after, but it feels so good when I'm doing it."

"I'm sure she knows you're just venting."

"I know she knows, but it doesn't make it right. But then I think I shouldn't have to worry about her. I'm the one dying. I should be able to do what I want if it feels good, right? A dying girl has the right, has that privilege, to be selfish."

"Tess, don't talk like that. You're not dying. You're just sick, like me."

"No, Tim, I'm not sick like you. You're getting better. Slowly, but better. Your tumor is shrinking. I'm getting worse. I haven't seen fresh air in nine months. You're living. I'm DYING!"

I fully understood the "quads envy paraplegics" line now. It *is* all about perspective. To healthy people, I seem very sick. But to dying people, I seem healthy.

"Tess, you're just in a bad cycle now. I'm sure—"

She interrupted. "Tim, I want to say this just once. So please listen." She took my hands, held my gaze with her eyes, and continued, "The doctors told me the treatments aren't working. They're trying new things, blah, blah, blah, but it's all just false hope. Am I hoping I live? Of course. But I have to also be a realist, and my reality is probably that…" She teared up at this moment, and her tears made me feel strong for her.

"How long?" I asked, sounding a lot like my dad.

She wiped her eyes with her arms and shrugged her shoulders.

"The winter?"

She shook her head no.

"Sooner?"

She nodded. Then she looked me in the eyes and the dam burst. She started sobbing these deep, guttural sobs I never thought a girl her size could produce. She threw her arms around my neck and buried her head in my chest. She was right on my broviac. I winced, but she couldn't see. I made a slight adjustment and just held her for a solid five minutes while she let it all out.

Finally, after a few last sniffles, she picked her head up and looked at me. "Let's just talk about anything other than being sick. That's what I want. That's what I need."

And for the next hour, she asked me questions about me. She mostly wanted to hear stories about me playing baseball. I told her some baseball stories: my best plays, my best games. She didn't know as much about baseball as I had thought. I told her all about my favorite Yankees— Don Mattingly, Ron Guidry, and, of course, Willie Randolph. I told her how I modeled my style of play after him.

She seemed enthralled—not because I was such a good storyteller, but, I suspect, because I was providing her an escape from her terrible reality. We were both smiling, Tess sitting in her chair and me on the edge of her bed, when our moms came back.

My mom said, "Timmy, we have to go now."

Tess asked, "When can he come back?"

Clara answered, "We'll try to do Wednesday and Friday afternoons. But Tess, dear, it depends on, ya know, how you're feeling."

Tess threw in, "You mean it depends if I'm alive."

Clara closed her eyes tightly and took in a deep breath, held it, and let it out slowly. Tess looked at me, smiled, and shrugged her shoulders while holding her palms out, implying that she couldn't help it.

Friday, August 17, 1984

This was my ninth visit this summer with Tess. We missed a few because she wasn't feeling well, and two because they were my Vincristine days. Each visit was like a therapy session. We'd sit for an hour or two and talk, one of us asking questions and the other answering questions. Last week's visit was especially rough for Tess because she'd missed Hobo Day. She hadn't achieved her goal.

Most of the time, we'd talk about things in my life. She got to know my family very well, and in a way, it was kind of cathartic for me. Finally, a week ago, I told her that this visit was going to be "Tess Day"—I wanted to hear only about her and her life back in Iowa. She hemmed and hawed for a few minutes but ultimately relented.

She told me all about her life in Iowa. She really lit up as she told me all about how she and her friends would actually hang out in the cemetery, reading the stones and making up stories, and how peaceful and cool it was.

I really got a taste for what Tess was like as she told me stories about hanging out uptown in the Candy Kitchen and Nissens Drug Store, drinking fountain sodas. She played a lot of tennis and climbed big, old trees, sitting high in the branches and trying out swear words like "damn" and, later on, more colorful, forbidden words.

She was a Girl Scout, and last summer, right before her diagnosis, she had gone for 12 days to an overnight camp in Clear Lake, Iowa. Her favorite part of that trip had been fishing in the lake. She told me she could fish for hours because she loved not knowing what was on the other end of the line. Imagination was under there.

It was beautiful to listen to her. I could totally picture Tess doing these things with a mixture of innocence and mischief.

Today, though, Tess was not herself. She spoke weakly, and her words were more breathy. She closed her eyes a lot and took deep breaths during sentences. She asked a lot about Victoria, but not in a jealous way. I believe she genuinely wanted to know about her. I told her all about the dance and the half-kiss.

"Do you want her to be your girlfriend?"

"I don't know. She's my friend, ya know? But so is Mike, and I certainly think about Victoria differently than Mike."

Tess laughed. "Maybe it's just your timing is off. I mean, like, when you get better, you guys can really be boyfriend-girlfriend instead of just pretending."

"I guess."

"Can I ask you a selfish question?"

"Yeah, Tess, what is it?"

"Can you wait until I'm gone to be her boyfriend? 'Cause right now, I like to think of you as *my* boyfriend."

"Tess, don't talk like—"

She shook me off, saying, "Let's not play that game today. It's a simple, selfish request. I want you all to myself while I'm here. When I'm gone, she can have you."

I just stared at her, and the more I paused, the deeper she looked into my eyes as though trying to command me to agree. At the same time, I saw her bottom lip start to quiver.

I took her hands in mine, looked right into her eyes, and said, "Of course. You're my girl, Tess. You're my girl." I kissed her on the forehead, then pulled back. She let go of my hands and put her hands on my shoulders. She slowly pulled me in; we tilted our heads and kissed on the lips. A few times.

When we stopped, she said, "I have one more request."

Smiling, I asked, "What now?"

"If you and Victoria grow up and get married, and if you have a daughter, can you name her Tess?"

Thursday, August 23, 1984

I didn't get to see Tess on Wednesday because I had to take my final exams. I passed them all. The tutors made it very easy for me—not that I needed their help on the tests, but they gave me help anyway (wink, wink). So, I'll be going to high school in a few weeks.

I told my parents that I'd like to go visit camp and see people. Camp ends tomorrow, and it has taken me almost the whole summer to get up the guts to visit, so I went today.

Dad and I got to camp at lunchtime. I put on a red Camp Keewee T-shirt and jeans, even though it was 90 degrees out. I wasn't comfortable with my pale, skinny legs. As soon as I stepped out of the car, a whole bunch of people came over to say hi. Seriously, I don't know why I get so self-conscious. Nobody seems to care what I look like other than me. They're all just happy to see me.

Ryan Miller came up to me and put his arm around my shoulder. Ryan is a very good friend and my biggest sports rival. Next year, he'll be going to my rival high school across town. Ever since we were eight years old, people have been talking about the potentially amazing match-ups and competitions between our future baseball teams. Ryan mockingly bragged about how he won all of this summer's trophies easily without me being there. We laughed, and he said, "See ya 'round."

My kindergarten camper buddies surrounded me, hugging my waist. One of them told me I looked weird. Gotta love the honesty of the young.

I saw some of the girls from last year's Alley-Oop party. They came over, gave me a hug, and said, "See ya 'round."

A friend of Evan's named Billy Weinstein came up to me and slapped me hard on the chest as he said, "Wow, man! Good to see you!" One of his fingers caught the clip of my broviac, and as he pulled his hand off my chest, it yanked the tube. I had a moment of panic that he had pulled it out of my chest and there'd be gushing blood everywhere, but he didn't. He just said, "Sorry, man. See ya 'round."

I stayed for about half an hour and then left. It was a good visit, and I realized that as a sick kid who is the center of attention, it's hard to remember that just because my life is on hold, everyone else's isn't. All the "See ya 'rounds" I heard today demonstrated that. They're moving on, leaving me behind. I'll either catch up to them and rejoin them or I won't. I'll get a new group to be a part of when I reenter the normal world. It's just life, and it's okay. On the way home, I made a mental note of this revelation so I could tell Tess at the next visit.

When I got home, Mom sat me down and told me that she just got a call that this morning, Tess died.

Friday, August 24, 1984

I haven't really cried yet. I've teared up a little, but I haven't bawled or wept. Maybe that's a result of being sick—you become a realist. Whether you see the glass as optimistically half-full or pessimistically half-empty doesn't really matter. Either way, the glass has to be washed.

Tess' funeral is going to be in Iowa on Sunday. We're not going. It's too far, too expensive. Mom and I went for a walk up our street this afternoon. We didn't say much. But at one point, Mom smiled, shook her head, and told me about her conversation with Tess's mom. She told me how during their brief conversation yesterday, she had said to Clara, "You must be so angry. I'm so sorry."

Mom said Clara's response was short and simple: "I am not angry. I don't question why Tess was taken from us at such an early age. I'm only thankful that I had her as long as I did." Mom thought that was beautiful.

Later, I had time to really think about everything. Lying on my bed, eyes closed, thoughts bouncing around in my head like Bingo balls in their cage hoping to be picked, I settled on this as the reason why I had been gifted this great summer with visits with Tess. What I learned from Tess was how to comfort. You comfort people on *their* terms, not yours. If they want to talk, you let them. If they want to listen, you talk to them. If they want a hug, you give it, and you don't stop until *they* let go. And if they just want a companion to sit silently with, be there. I suspect this is a skill that will come in handy many times in the future. Maybe I'm wrong, but for now, that thought comfort me.

I took a baseball out of my gym bag. On it, I drew a heart, and inside the heart, I put:

I put the ball in a shoebox with her letters and her pictures, and put the shoebox on my windowsill. It took me a while, but eventually, I fell asleep.

Wednesday, September 5, 1984

Last Friday, I got my freshman-year schedule in the mail. Yesterday, the day before school started, Mom, Evan, Jeremy, and I had gone to the high school to talk with my teachers. Evan and Jeremy ran around the halls while Mom and I met each teacher individually. The agenda of these talks was to let them know my condition (which they all knew about, by the way) and inform them that every few weeks I'd be missing school for what was hopefully going to be my last cycle of chemo. In fact, my doctor said everything was looking swell (he had actually used that word) and that if everything continued to go well, I should be done with my chemo treatments in January.

After I met all my teachers, Mom took Jeremy home. Evan and I stayed at the school so he could give me a tour of the place. He showed me all around the school, told me funny stories, warned me about which kids I should be wary of and where not to hang out, like the courtyard. It was a great talk. A solid hour of bonding with Evan.

Evan had gotten his driver's license over the summer. While he was driving me home, he threw this out at me: "If anyone gives you a problem, you let me know. I'll take care of it."

"Okay. But I think I'll be okay."

"I know you think that. And you probably will. But you let me know if things happen. You promise?"

"Yeah, I promise."

"Good."

I'm not sure what Evan could do to help. He's not necessarily a tough guy. But he does have influence. He's very popular, and as far as I know, he has no enemies, so his vow to protect me made me feel a little more secure.

Mike got back from football camp and looks even bigger than when he left. He is so confident about high school. I imagine I would be, too, if I were a freshman who is virtually a lock for the varsity football team.

We spoke on the phone last night. At one point, Mike brought up a weird conversation. "Hey, Tim. Listen. I'm going to be sitting with the football team at lunch. One of the varsity guys was at the camp, and he told me it would be to my benefit to sit with them."

"Wow, that's awesome, Mike. That's great!" But I guess I didn't sound too convincing.

"You'll have people to sit with. Don't sweat it."

"I'm not worried."

"Just know this doesn't change anything between you and me. I always got your back, Tim. You know that, right?"

"Yeah, man. Of course."

"We've been friends for too long to stop now," he assured us both. So now I have two protectors. I know that should make me feel good and boost my confidence, and it does, but it also makes me feel small, which I am. There is also a jealousy factor going on. I should be sitting with the baseball team, fitting in with those guys, instead of sitting with...I don't even know.

And I'm not worried that Mike and I won't be friends anymore. I fully accept that we have to find our own paths. But I know he'll be there if I need him. This is how I know:

Last year, we had been playing a summer league baseball game. Mike was catching, and I was playing second base. We were up by one run, and the other team was up, last licks. They had a runner on first, with two outs. The batter hit a deep fly ball to right center. Our left fielder, Lance Behnke, dove and missed it. As the ball rolled to the fence, the runner rounded second and flew to third. Our center fielder, Pat Breen, backing up Lance, got the ball and threw it to me, the cutoff man. Although my back was to him, I heard Mike yelling, "Throw home! Throw home!" as the runner rounded third. I caught the cutoff and whipped around to throw home to Mike. I didn't have a good grip on the ball, and I threw it short and to the first-base side of home plate. Mike made an amazing scoop and tagged the runner, who was trying to slide to the back of home plate. He was out, and we won. It was Mike who totally made that play.

Afterward, a reporter from our local newspaper interviewed Mike about the play. The way Mike told the story, the throw from me had been perfect and Mike had bobbled it, only to recover just in time. Mike talked me up, even though I was the one who almost blew it. Mike never made me look bad. He knew that it was more important for me to look good in the paper than for him because he was more of a football guy. He had given up the glory for me. That's sacrifice. That's a true friend.

I know I keep harping on this, but I felt really small and self-conscious the first day of high school. I sensed a lot of people staring at me and whispering. At the same time, I had various friends of Evan's come up to me and pat me on the back or walk next to me. Some of his girl friends gave me hello hugs in the hallway. I know how Evan works. This was his way of sending a message to the general public that I am not one to be messed with. I was so grateful.

At lunch, I stood on line with Mike to get our cheeseburgers. After we paid, he looked at me and paused. He was waiting for me to free him to sit with his football boys. I gave him the silent nod. He gave me a half-smile, half-smirk of thanks. I was happy for him. I was also very envious of him. He left me in a situation I'd never been in before. Where do I sit for lunch? Who do I sit with?

It's not easy trying to walk around a cafeteria, looking nonchalantly for someone to sit with while feeling terrified inside. I finally spotted a table in a corner with five other freshmen—two boys and three girls. I knew them but wasn't friends with them. One of the girls, Lois, called me over. "Tim, we have room. You want to sit?"

"Sure, thanks." I sat down. "Lois, right?"

"Yes. I'm Lois. We were in gym together in seventh and eighth grade—well, seventh grade." She blushed, realizing the awkwardness of the moment.

I laughed to ease her out of it. "I know. I remember. And you're Tracy and Lori." I turned to the guys. "Mark Grossman and Dave Becker, right?"

The girls smiled politely, and Mark said, "Tim Levine. Glad you're here. I mean, here in *school*, not here, like, on the planet as opposed to dead. You know what I mean!"

We all laughed at Mark's awkwardness and, just like that, I found a comfort zone. It also helped that more of Evan's friends came over to say hi. Evan didn't. He knew I had to do this myself. But still, I knew he had orchestrated it.

And although I was feeling pretty good, I still heard whispers and felt stares.

Friday, September 14, 1984

So this is how the other half lives. After a week of school, a week of having lunch with my new "crew," I've become very aware of life as an outsider. Outsider is too nice of a word. It's hard for me to admit, but my new friends are dorky. They aren't geeks. Geeks are weirdos with unwashed hair and mismatched clothes. They have too much interest in Dungeons and Dragons, and a knack for making up song parodies that are nowhere near funny to anyone other than them.

Dorky kids, like my new table of friends, are normal, but a few cool experiences away from being popular. These guys loved to talk about how dorky they were. They enjoyed telling me that none of them have ever kissed someone of the opposite gender. They laughed as they shared stories about their athletic ineptitude. They didn't bemoan the fact that they weren't popular. They embraced their spot in the social hierarchy. In a weird way, their acceptance gave them confidence—except when in the presence of the cool, popular kids.

They loved that I was a cool, popular kid who was now "slumming" with them. That's what Mark called it. He told us how his older sister went to the same college as the quarterback of our high school team from two years ago. She had been a regular, plain-Jane girl in high school, but college was a clean slate. Now she was the popular sorority girl, while the once-quarterback was now kind of a loner who kept trying to hang out with her, despite the fact that two years earlier in high school, he hadn't given her so much as a glance in the hallway.

My new crew all seem pretty aware that I may be just biding my time with them until the day when I rejoin the popular group. But they also know that I need them right now. I need them because I need to be with people who understand not quite fitting in; I need to learn what it feels like to not get invited everywhere. These are things they know very well.

And they love my stories of the "in" crowd. They can't believe that not only had I made out with Stephanie Frezza, who is infinitely hotter this year compared to last year, but that I had turned her down. They loved hearing about the athletic scene and about me hanging with all the athletes. Tracy and Lori's eyes widened as I told them about Mike and some others—guys they've had crushes on for years but had never had the nerve to talk to.

It's like we've come to an unspoken understanding. We need each other.

But aside from all of that, and most important, I generally liked this crew. They were very nonjudgmental of people and very accepting of people's flaws—not that my athlete friends weren't—at least so I thought. But Thursday at lunch, Lois had told a story about how, in fifth grade, she had made the mistake of saying "the EREC-

TION of President Reagan" instead of "the ELECTION of President Reagan" during social studies. As she told the story, I could tell she got the humor of her verbal error, but I saw in her eyes how she had been hurt because for the next year, everyone called her Boner. She held my gaze for an extra moment as I came to the realization that I had started that nickname. I remembered the incident instantly and felt terribly ashamed.

I looked away from Lois momentarily, but when I made eye contact again, she let me off the hook with a lips-closed smile as she said, "That was four years ago. The next year, we went to middle school and most people forgot. No big deal. I'm over it."

But I could tell she wasn't, nor would she ever completely be. I was the one—not on purpose, but still definitely at fault—who had relegated her to "dork" status in fifth grade and sentenced her to it possibly through to college. And yet here she was, completely accepting of me when I am down. There's beauty in that. Each one of them had it in his or her own way. It's what drew me to them and made me stay friends with them until we graduated and beyond.

"I'm going to the football game tonight against Mahopac. Mike might get in a few special teams plays. You guys want to go?"

"To the football game?" Dave asked incredulously.

"Well, yeah, Dave. We can meet at the gym doors, and we'll walk up to the field together. My brother's saving a bench near the front of the bleachers."

They all agreed.

Evan and I drove to the game together. I told him I'd meet him after I met my friends. I watched all of them get dropped off by their parents. I was wearing jeans and an extra-large Yankees T-shirt. I still have to wear oversized tops because of my broviac, but I think I looked cool enough, except for my stupid wig. Mark was wearing floods, his light khaki pants about three inches above his sneakers. He and Dave wore matching Lakeland High School Drama Club jackets, as did Lois. Tracy and Lori wore their hair the same—in long ponytails with multicolored barrettes that made them look like middle school kids. I could tell they tried hard to look good but just fell short.

As we walked to our seats, a lot of people came to say hi to me. Stephanie came up to me and gave me a kiss on the cheek before she walked away with her new senior boyfriend, their hands in each other's back pockets.

Right before the game started, I brought my friends down to the fence bordering the field and yelled to Mike. He jogged over in his uniform, and we chatted for a moment. I introduced him to my new friends.

"Nice to meet you. Very cool of you to come and show support." He turned to me. "I look good, don't I?"

"Dude, you look awesome. Do some damage out there. Good luck, my man."

Mike and I high-fived. Tracy and Lori were swooning over him. I rolled my eyes.

As Mike ran to his team, he looked back at me and mouthed, "Boner?" I smiled, shrugged my shoulders, and laughed, as did he.

I spent most of the first quarter explaining the game of football to Mark, Lois, and Tracy. It was astounding to me how little they knew. Dave and Lori tried to out-debate each other about who was better, the Jets or the Giants. At one point, I was able to sit back and reflect, and I felt comfortable in where I was at the moment, kind of stuck between stations in life. Meeting new friends, keeping the old. I thought of that silly Girl Scout song:

Make new friends, but keep the old.
One is silver, and the other's gold.

I was generally happy. Even knowing I was going into the hospital the next week for what I hoped was my last inpatient week, I was feeling good. I was seeing a light at the end of the tunnel.

At halftime, I saw Victoria. She was walking back from the hot dog stand with her older sister. I followed her with my eyes all the way to her seat. Her hair had gotten longer, and I'm pretty sure she looked taller. She looked cute. Very Victoriaesque—which is to say very average, but cute-average. She is definitely not a stunner, but I'd guess—correctly, by the way—that by senior year, she would be.

I stood up so she could see me, and I waved her over to us. She and I hugged, a very plain, ordinary, just-two-friends hug—quick, with no lingering feelings or awkwardness. It seems any chemistry we had felt after the dance had vanished like a card in a magic trick. For now, it's fine. Like Tess said, our timing is off. I need friends now.

Victoria knew my crew—not well, but she knew them. Fit right in, actually.

"It's good to see you, Tim. How are you feeling?"

"Good. You know. I still have a few months to go, but overall, pretty good."

We continued with small talk, and the seven of us enjoyed the next two hours watching the game and just hanging out. Our team lost 24-10.

Mike got in the game for three plays, all punt returns. He missed an easy open-field tackle on his first play that would have pinned Mahopac on its own five-yard line. Some guys get down on themselves when they miss a play; they shuffle back to the bench or dugout, shake their heads, and sulk in the corner of the bench. Not Mike. Head held high, he jogged back to the bench and mentally kept himself in the game, just waiting for redemption.

Two series later, he got it. As our punter kicked the ball high in the air, Mike eluded the first wave of blockers and met the punt returner just as he caught the ball. With a hard shoulder hit to the returner's hands, Mike dislodged the ball. Dave Keylin, a senior, picked up the fumble and ran it into the end zone for our only touchdown.

At the end of the game, I saw the team taking a knee in a huddle on the sideline, some with arms draped around each other as the coach gave them a quick post-game talk before heading into the locker room. I watched and was happy for Mike, but it made me miss that camaraderie. I looked at my new crew, then back at the football team. I felt pangs of anger and regret. It' be a huge blow to my psyche if I don't get a chance to have that competitive feeling again, to have that teammate bond again. I don't know if I'll make it back in time to play baseball. I don't know if I'll ever have that again.

Thursday, September 20, 1984

It's less than a month from my one-year anniversary of being diagnosed with cancer. I spent the week as an inpatient—, hopefully the last week as an inpatient. After this, I just have sporadic outpatient chemo days until January 17, my last scheduled chemo treatment.

Tuesday was my last Vincristine day. Watching the 61st drip, the last "make-me-feel-good" drip before the bad ones started taking over, I rolled onto my side into my usual fetal position facing my mom. I looked up at her, both of us smiling, and she said, "I'm starting to see an end to all of this."

I nodded, but I have a lot of my dad's realism in me. I love how Mom is so optimistic about everything, but I hate the look of disappointment she often gets from being overly optimistic and then having things turn out not so well. I've learned from my dad to hope for the best but prepare for the worst. If you expect the worst and it turns out well, it's a pleasant surprise.

So I didn't respond to Mom, but I hope she saw in my eyes how I appreciated her optimism. I hope I was able to convey that before I started puking.

On the pediatric floor of Sloan Kettering, every milestone is cause for celebration. At the end of the day, when I was feeling up to it, Jack the Clown came by. Actually, it was just Jack. No makeup. No shtick. He brought balloons and a gift-wrapped present.

"Congrats! No more Vincristine, buddy! Let's celebrate!" He brought out a bottle of champagne. My eyes widened.

"It's not for you, punk. It's for your mom." He handed it to her, gave her a kiss on the cheek, and then turned to me. He handed me the gift. "Look," he said, "it's been a pleasure to get to know you, my man. And it's really nice to be able to say good-bye for a good reason. Unfortunately, it's not always that way." He paused, and I know we both thought about Tess for a moment. "So on the occasion that it is a positive farewell, presents are in order. Go ahead, dude. Open it up."

I ripped open the wrapping paper and saw a framed picture of Willie Randolph, my favorite Yankee, in midair, turning a double play. Then I saw it was a *signed* framed picture of Willie Randolph. Then I saw it was signed specifically to *me* by Willie Randolph. It said, "Dear Tim, So glad you're feeling better. Think positive and don't let the bad hops beat you. Willie Randolph #30."

"How the heck did this happen?" I asked incredulously.

"Willie and a few other Yankees came by to see the inpatients two weeks ago. I knew you'd be back here soon, so I got him to sign for ya."

My eyes filled with tears, held in momentarily by cohesion (I looked it up); when I blinked, they raced down my face. I think it was Jack's kindness combined with the realization that I'd never see him again. Oh yeah, and the fact that I had a personalized Willie Randolph signed picture!

"Thank you, Jack," I mumbled between tears. I leaned in to hug him.

Jack rubbed my bald head as I heard my mom, teary herself, saying, "Yes, Jack, thank you. For everything."

"My pleasure. It's what I do. Now Tim, you need to make me a promise."

"Sure. Anything."

"Not an empty promise. You have to come through on this."

"What is it?"

"You have to promise that when you get older, you will come back here and volunteer your time to help other kids be happy. And if you live somewhere else in the country, you have to volunteer at a local hospital. You promise?"

"I don't know about the clown thing, Jack."

"You don't have to be a clown. There are many other things you can do."

I put my hand out, and we shook on it. Then he pulled out of his pocket a picture of a little bald boy sitting on a hospital bed. He held it up next to his face and smiled exactly the same way as the boy in the picture.

"Oh man, is that you?" I asked.

Jack nodded. "Twenty-one years ago. That was me."

"It's a deal. I promise," I said.

"Alright, my man. I'm out. Be good."

"Bye, Jack."

As he left, I knew instantly that I would fulfill my promise. And that I would probably be a clown.

Tomorrow I go home. Like Mom said on Tuesday, I do see a finish line. I can hear the famous horse race call "And DOWN the stretch they come!" I am cautiously optimistic, though, because although I am ready to sprint to the finish line, I know that sometimes a horse stumbles and limps across it—or doesn't cross it at all.

Wednesday, November 7, 1984

I got sent to the principal's office. For the life of me, I couldn't think what I had done wrong. Turns out Mr. Robinson, the bowling coach, wanted to see me.

We met in the assistant principal's office. Mr. Robinson stood and put out his hand to shake mine. He is a very large, bulky man and looks like he should be the football coach, not the bowling coach. His hand completely enveloped mine when we shook hands, similar to the professional wrestlers' hands had. Maybe that's why he's the bowling coach—he's got the big hand to control the ball.

"Tim, it's nice to meet you. I hear you're an excellent baseball player."

"Thank you, sir."

"Mr. Villone called me and told me about your situation and that you'll be away from baseball for a while."

"It looks that way."

"I coach the bowling team. Are you interested in trying out?"

"Yes, I am," I answered without hesitation. It may not be baseball, but it's kind of a sport. And I liked this guy.

"Good. I just got off the phone with your dad. He approves. Barring a note from your doctor saying you can't, welcome to the Lakeland High School Bowling Team."

"Thanks, Mr. Robinson."

"Call me Coach."

I laughed. I didn't mean to. It just seems weird. Coaches coach football and baseball and hockey. People bowl.

He caught my vibe. "We take this seriously, and it gets competitive. We made it to the county semis two years in a row, and we're hoping to make the jump to the finals this year. If you commit, it's got to be full-on. Understand?"

"Yes, Coach. I do."

"Good. Come Saturday to a practice, and we'll see what you got. Maybe try to get you into a match game sooner rather than later."

We spoke for a few more minutes. He told me that it's a complete mix of students on the team. Anyone can start, freshman through senior. Like in wrestling, there is a bowl-off on the day before a match. The six highest scores compete varsity; the rest competed JV. With 11 guys on the team, there is almost a 50% chance I'd roll varsity. Sounded like good odds to me.

That night after dinner, Dad gave me an unwrapped box.

"Open it."

With my whole family sitting around, I opened the box. Inside was a forest green jacket with gold stripes along the neck collar and wrists. As I lifted it, I saw it was a Lakeland varsity jacket. On the front left side was my name with two bowling pins crisscrossed underneath it sewed on in yellow. On the back was "Lakeland" rainbowed across the top and "Bowling" reverse-rainbowed on the bottom, with a bowling ball smashing through pins in the middle.

I looked around. Dad and Mom were beaming. They were genuinely proud of me.

Evan was smirking, acknowledging the un-coolness of wearing a varsity bowling jacket. "It's kinda dorky, but at least it's not a chess team jacket," he said.

I put the jacket on. It was way too big. There was no way I could actually wear it in public. But I don't think that mattered. What mattered was what the jacket represented. It represented two futures for me—*a* future, and an *athletic* future.

Monday, December 3, 1984

My 14th birthday. Lori and Victoria baked cupcakes for the seven of us at the lunch table. Dave brought in party hats, and as he started to put one on, we all looked at him until he recognized that that was probably a little too dorky and removed it. Mark gave me a Yankees banner. The girls had all chipped in and bought me a Bryan Adams cassette. I would have listened to it right then in Lori's Walkman, but the Walkman was not a good match for my wig.

Mark turned to Dave. "What'd you get for Tim?"

"Umm, just these party hats."

We all laughed. As I was laughing, I noticed that along the back wall of the cafeteria, about three tables away, sitting on the radiator, were a bunch of juniors. The radiator is where the older students hung. It's a place to be seen because anyone there was physically above the students at the tables. The radiator was populated by mostly juniors because the seniors usually went out for lunch. Evan's jock crew and some other preppy kids usually sit at the far end of the cafeteria from where my table is located. It was seen as a symbol of good standing if a sophomore or freshman was allowed to sit with the juniors on the radiator. Symbolically, Evan had brought me there for five minutes on the third day of school. This really impressed my crew. Evan hasn't brought me back since. No more nepotism.

On the close end of the radiator, near where we sit, were the juniors who smoked, wore jean jackets with black Black Sabbath shirts, and high leather boots even on the hot days of September and June. They mostly had long hair and were known as burnouts. It was a social class, like jock or nerd. The burnouts were interesting. They probably would have been popular like the jocks if they'd had any athleticism. They were seen as mostly cool, as long as no one messed with them. The perception was that they probably all did drugs; thus, the title. I don't know if that's true. It's just their reputation.

A small percentage of burnouts were very uncool. They went out of their way to intimidate and grab attention in a negative way. They were the type to cut in front of you on the lunch line and knock your tray over if you shot them a look. Basically, they were the bullies of the school.

So as I was laughing at Dave's gift miscalculation, I noticed one of the burnouts staring at me funny. Then he whispered to his friends and stared at me again. It made me very uncomfortable. I tried to ignore him, but in my peripheral vision, I kept seeing him doing it. Then I saw him get up off the radiator and walk toward me. I swallowed hard and tried to engross myself in table conversation and ignore him. I couldn't. I looked back over but didn't see him anymore. Thank God, he left—or so I thought. All of a sudden, I felt a hand slap the side of my head and lift up a corner of my wig. I cowered, and the kid walked behind me, back to the radiator. Apparently, he noticed my wig and was trying to knock it off. I saw him laughing, pointing, and telling his buddies.

The whole thing happened fast, and I don't even think anyone at my table knew. They probably thought he bumped into me by accident. But I knew. I looked at the kid and immediately knew two things. First, I recognized the kid. He was Nick Brownstone. We had been on the same baseball team for two years in elementary school until he had gotten too old and moved to an older league. We had been friendly as teammates. He became a burnout, and today, he didn't recognize me—understandable because I look so different, unfortunate because he'd become a bully burnout and I was his latest victim. Second, I knew he was coming back for another try, as his friends started egging him on.

I looked to the other side of the cafeteria, hoping to catch a glimpse of Evan or one of his friends. I didn't see any of them. I did, though, see Nick Brownstone coming back for round two. I didn't know what to do. I didn't want to get up and leave, for fear of antagonizing him. I also thought I would be safer here in the cafeteria, assuming—*hoping*—he wouldn't have the guts to do anything too harsh in front of everyone. So I sat and prayed he would just pass by. He didn't. This time, he slapped me on the back of my head with an upward motion. My wig moved forward and covered my eyes. I quickly adjusted it as Nick went back to the radiator, laughing and falling all over his buddies.

This time, my table of friends knew. I looked each one in the eyes. They stared back at me, not saying a word. I was about four seconds away from crying. I mean all-out, tears-flowing, chest-heaving sobbing. I honestly didn't know which would be worse—the wig flying off or me crying in the cafeteria. I got up and exited through the door. I made a quick left and stood against the window in the empty hallway.

I was mortified. I was devastated. That damn wig! My stomach ached as if I'd been punched. My face was beet red. And the tears came. I could control the sobbing, but I couldn't control the tears. I knew that any second, the bell would ring, the cafeteria would empty, and everyone would see me crying. I wanted to run to the bathroom or the office, but my legs were frozen. I thought this must be what it feels like to be a deer frozen in the headlights—you know you have to move, but you just can't.

The cafeteria doors opened, and I prepared for the worst moment of my life. I looked away, and a moment later, I felt a soft hand on my bicep. It was Lois. Tracy, Lori, Victoria, Dave, and Mark stood behind her. She gave me a small nod and a small smile. She'd been in this position before. Slowly, they formed a semicircle around me, facing away, shielding me as the bell rang and students poured into the hallway. Effectively shielded from the crowd by my friends, the tears came, and they came hard.

Two minutes later, the hallway cleared and the tears stopped. I could only muster, "Thanks."

Victoria squeezed my hand, and they all walked away.

Happy birthday to me.

Friday, January 18, 1985

We've had five bowling matches so far. I rolled varsity in one, the latest one. In the bowl-off, I rolled one pin higher than the sixth-best guy on the team, which then made me the sixth-best bowler. Before that, I'd been averaging around 150. That day, I bowled a 188—not great, but good enough for the sixth slot.

The bowling team is an interesting group. We have two hard-core bowlers who consistently bowl in the 220s. They are seniors, twins, Donald and Randy, and they wear the arm-wrist brace that professionals wear. They have the same style—a four-step approach, long extension toward the gutter, with a quick inward turn of the wrist at the apex of their release. Their balls spin madly toward the gutter halfway down the lane, hover on the precipice for what seems like forever, and then turn angrily toward the pocket at a sharp angle. The pins explode every time. It's beautiful to watch, really. Donald is a lefty, and Randy is a righty. Sometimes in practice, they bowl together on the same lane, Donald's ball skimming the left gutter, Randy's skimming the right. Both balls turn at exactly the same moment and crash into each pocket simultaneously. It must be cool being a twin.

Our number-three bowler is Robby Cannone, also known as The Cannon. He is strictly a strength guy. He was the backup tight end on the football team until he broke his left elbow. Now he throws the ball straight down the middle at a maddening speed. He seems to release major amounts of anger on each throw. He consistently averages a 200.

Numbers four and five, Vernon Meisner and Kyle Basini, are fat kids, not well groomed, who seem to have found the one thing they can be proud of themselves for. They average in the 190s.

And, at least for now, I'm the sixth man. I'm a handshake bowler. That means I line up two arrows right of center and throw the ball straight, turning my wrist as if I'm shaking hands with the pins. This gives me just the right amount of curve to hit the pocket. My weakness is my weakness. The pins don't explode like they should. And after a game and a half, my arm gets tired and my ball ends up drifting to the right.

In my first varsity match, I bowled a 198, a 168, and then a 161. Coach Robinson liked what he saw, gave me a few pointers, and told me I have potential.

It's a decent group of kids.   We high-five a lot.
They've taught me bowling jargon, like three strikes in a
row is a turkey. If all but one guy gets a strike in the same
frame, it's a Coke frame, and the one guy who didn't strike
buys a round of Cokes. If you leave only the five pin standing, that's the make out pin. That means you won't make
out with a girl for at least five weeks. The only way to nul-
lify a make out jinx is to roll a spare the next time you have
the five pin standing alone. Stupid things, I know, but they
keep everyone laughing, having a good time.

And believe it or not, there is competition and pressure! A few weeks before, the match was tied and it came
down to the final bowler for each team. The other guy hit
two strikes and a seven in his 10th frame. For us, it fell on
Kyle Basini. He got the first strike. The whole alley went
quiet.   He tentatively got in position, made a slow
approach, and released. It was a perfect spin into the
pocket for strike two. Our team started stamping and
pounding on the benches, whooping it up. As Kyle
approached for his final roll, again, complete alley silence.
Kyle was actually sweating. I looked around and saw that
the bowlers took this just as seriously as I did in the bottom
of the ninth or as Mike did during an overtime field goal
attempt.

Kyle took a deep breath and rolled a nine, leaving just
the make out pin. We won, and it felt very gratifying,
being in the middle of some good ol' competitive fire
again.

Incidentally, if you finish a game that you win and
leave the make out pin, supposedly, you will make out with
someone within 24 hours. Looking at Kyle, I highly doubt
it. But hey, ya never know!

Yesterday morning was my last chemo treatment. My
parents, three doctors, and five nurses gathered around for

the occasion. The nurse let me administer it to myself. I lifted the broviac, inserted the syringe filled with the red chemo called Adriamycin into the tip, snapped out the air bubbles, and slowly pushed it into my body. As I did, the doctors and nurses were all pumping their fists and chanting, "Go! Go! Go! Go!" My dad laughed and said it reminded him of college. I looked at him quizzically, and he winked.

"You'll understand in a few years."

When I finished with the syringe, everyone cheered. Mom cried. The nurses kissed my forehead and cheek. The doctors patted my leg and back. It was a corny moment, but I loved it.

After all the hoopla, we sat with Dr. Santiago, a tiny, Filipina woman who had been my main doctor for this last cycle. She explained a lot of things to us. About an hour after my last injection, they took a final CAT scan of my head. Dr. Santiago explained that if all looked good, I would have my broviac taken out. I looked at Dad, alarmed.

"No, Tim. They're not going to rip this one out."

"That's right," Dr. Santiago concurred. "We'll put you under and remove it surgically. It's about an hour-long process. We'll keep you overnight to watch for infection."

Then she told us that I am now officially in remission and after five years in remission, I could consider myself cured.

Dr. Santiago put her hands on my cheeks and held my head. "You are no longer a cancer patient, young man. You're a cancer survivor."

With that, Mom broke down. Dad consoled her, and for the first time, I saw my dad cry. It's like he'd held everything in for the past 15 months, staying strong for all of us. The rush of joy and relief finally brought him to tears. It was beautiful to witness.

Dr. Santiago also told us I have to come back every six months for a CAT scan, chest X-ray, and blood work. After five years of that, I come back once a year for the rest of my life.

Dr. Santiago concluded, "And in about four months, your hair will start growing back."

I got home today. Mike was at my house with his parents. Evan, Jeremy, and he had put up a banner over our garage. It had a picture of a bowling ball with my name on it smashing into the pins, each of which said, "Cancer." Underneath the picture, the banner said, "Cancer strikes out!" and under that, "Welcome Back to Normal."

Mike's family stayed another hour for drinks and desserts. When they left, Mom told us that our rabbi rescheduled my bar mitzvah for June 1. It was only four and a half months away, so I'd be studying with him every Saturday after services and once during the week for two hours after school.

I started to get tired. I went upstairs, got undressed, and stood in front of the mirror in my underwear. I assessed myself. I have a round scar where the gastrostomy tube was. It looks like I have two belly buttons. I have a bandage on my chest; underneath it will be a scar that, according to Dr. Santiago, will probably be very small and, with any luck, eventually covered with chest hair. I still have no arm or leg hair. No eyebrows or eyelids. No hair on my head. I have very pale skin, except for the discoloration on my face from the radiation. I have the body of a 10-year-old boy. I look pathetic. But this time, I feel good about myself. Sure, my hair is still gone, but it will come back. The cancer was gone now. And, God willing, it ain't coming back. I have my life back!

Thursday, March 14, 1985

Tonight was the awards dinner for the varsity sports. Each team sat together at its own table. The football team went first. Each varsity player gets called up individually and is given a gold letter L by his or her coach. When Mike was called up, I could tell he was proud. I was happy for him. He only played special teams this season, but he returned a fumble on a punt return for a touchdown. It was the first time a freshman had ever done that in our school history.

We sat through boys and girls soccer, field hockey, swimming, gymnastics, and lacrosse, and then it was the bowling team's turn. Coach Robinson called me last. As I started walking up to get my letter, I heard Mike yell from across the room, "Yeah, Tim!" He stood up and started clapping. Then slowly, the rest of the football team stood up with him.

Evan was sitting with the baseball team. They all stood up. One by one, each team rose and gave me a standing ovation. I looked at Evan, who winked at me. I looked at the varsity baseball coach, who mouthed, "Next year," as he pointed to his baseball team.

Coach Robinson handed me my gold L. I shook his hand. "Ya know," he said, "bowling and baseball are different seasons. You can do both."

I smiled up at him, grateful. I looked at the crowd and motioned for them to stop. I felt silly. I felt undeserving of a standing ovation. I sat back down sheepishly, feeling very flattered as the baseball team, wrestling team, cheerleaders, and track teams all got their turn getting their letters.

I always knew I'd get a varsity letter as a freshman. Never in a million years, though, would I have guessed it would be as a bowler, not a baseball player.

Saturday, June 1, 1985

Here's the thing about bar mitzvahs: 100% of the kids and 90% of the adults don't give a crap about the service. They all just want to go to the party. This is universal, whether you're Jewish or not. Everyone just waits out the service, as a duty to earn the right to go and party afterward.

During the first hour and a half of the service, I sang only four songs. And three of those, I really sang just the first line for. After the first line, the congregation joined in and I could fake the rest. Then at 10:45, it was time for me to become a man, a year and a half late. I sang the opening prayer and launched into my haftorah. It was about two and a half pages of Hebrew, which I chanted flawlessly even though I didn't understand one word of what I was saying— a standard practice among bar and bat mitzvah kids.

As I sang the closing prayer, I looked up and saw I actually had the attention of most people. A few younger cousins were hitting each other, and a great uncle I've met maybe once was sleeping. But mostly, everyone was watching. My mom had tears in her eyes as she held Dad's hand in her lap. I know they were proud of me, but I also know they thought that there was a good chance this wasn't ever going to happen.

The sisterhood and men's club gave brief, generic speeches about "finding my path" and "continuing my Jewish education," and so on. They gave me symbolic gifts—my own personal pocket torah and my own prayer book. Hug, kiss on the cheek, and then it was my turn for my speech.

I gathered myself, took a deep breath, and surveyed the crowd. This was my batting ritual, and I did it instinctively—a quick assessment of the scene before stepping into the batter's box and letting it rip.

"I just read from the Torah, and I led the service today at my bar mitzvah. I have to admit, I don't understand the translation of what I read. I don't understand the meaning. So I've come up with my own meaning of what my bar mitzvah means to me."

I continued, "For me, it means that all the people that are special to me, that I love and who love me, including friends and family, are here today to celebrate my 'becoming a man.'" I put my hands up and mimed quotation marks as I said that. I looked up and caught Mike's eyes as he made a muscle, mocking me. I so wanted to give him the finger, but I just smiled.

I took a deep breath, then continued, "I looked in the mirror this morning, and I didn't look like a man. I looked like a little boy. I don't necessarily feel like a man, either. But I think I know what it *means* to become a man. It means that you are proud of yourself, and of who you are, regardless of what others may think. You set goals and you accomplish them. Well, this being my bar mitzvah, my goal is to start becoming a man. And the best thing I can think to do at the moment is to be proud to do something I should have done months ago but didn't because I was ashamed."

Here I paused and walked out from behind the podium. I walked to the middle of the stage, looked around, and reached up, slowly taking my wig off, revealing a very short sprouting of peach-fuzz hair. A mixture of gasps, chuckles, cheers, and applause followed. I reached up and rubbed my head.

"Becoming a man," I said proudly. "Step one."

A bar mitzvah party is very different with 14- and 15-year-olds than it is with 12- and 13-year-olds. We played the same games, but you can be sure that during the limbo contest, all eyes were watching down a girl's dress while she was arched back at practically 90 degrees. And there were many more boy-girl partners during Coke and Pepsi, with much more aggressive sitting.

The dancing was different, too. Especially the slow dancing. The 12- and 13-year-olds dance with the boy's hands on the girl's hips and the girl's hands on the boy's shoulders, regardless of height differential. There is a three-foot cushion of air between the dancers, and no eye contact.

The 14- and 15-year olds dance with the boy's arms around the girl's waist, hands clasped on her back, just above her butt and with the girl's hands clasped around the boy's neck, with minimal space between the dancers, and full-on eye contact, as well as some whispering in the ears.

After the initial round of dancing, the bandleader brought out the cake for the candle-lighting service. This is where I say a silly little poem, introducing people as they come up to light a candle while the bandleader plays a song and the guests clap to a Hava Nagila" beat:

> "They flew all the way from Chicago to be here with me;
> Aunt Mari and Uncle Arthur, come light candle number three."

> "Although mostly big jerks, I guess they're fine;
> Evan and Jeremy, come light candle number nine."

Corny, I know, but it seems to work. For the last candle, I motioned for the bandleader to quiet everyone down.

"This last candle is for someone special, as were all the others, but this person couldn't be here today. She helped me more than I thought possible, and I will never forget her. This candle is for you, Tess."

I lit it amongst whispers of, "Who's that?" and "What's he talkin' about?" I looked at Mom, and she nodded. I nodded back. I wish Tess could have been here.

Unfortunately for me, while my friends went back to dancing close and were on the verge of making out (in fact, rumor has it that Mark and Lori made out in the lobby and Mike made out with my 17-year-old cousin), I was mostly occupied with taking pictures, talking with relatives, and letting people rub my newly sprouted hair.

Finally, after we all devoured the dessert bar, there was one last slow dance. I found Victoria sitting with her heels off, talking with Tracy.

"Would you like to dance?" I asked her.

"Of course. 'Bout time you asked me!" She and Tracy exchanged a little girl giggle. Victoria moved to put her shoes on.

"Leave them off. It'll work better."

I held her hand, and we went to the middle of the dance floor. I saw Mike. He gave me a thumbs-up and mouthed the words, "We're back." I nodded and faced Victoria. We stepped in toward each other, but with Victoria being a good five to six inches taller than me, we recognized the awkwardness of the pose and stepped apart a little. We didn't say much at first, just moved our hips and stepped back and forth, like 12-year-olds.

"Victoria, thanks for everything. You've been great. A great friend."

"I'm just so happy that you are where you are right now."

"Me, too." I smiled, not sure if she meant that suggestively or not. Probably not.

"Ya know, Tim, I'm not going to sleep-away camp this summer. So I'll be home and looking for something to do."

"I don't think I'm going to Keewee this year. I kinda had enough of that."

"Really?"

"Yeah. Which means I'll be around, too, looking for something to do."

We stared into each other. And even though the song was ending and the day was coming to a close, I had the feeling that this was just the beginning. I had my life back, and I was ready to begin.

LaVergne, TN USA
06 April 2011
223185LV00001B/2/P